## Meredith wanted him, but knew she couldn't have him.

Seeing her hesitate, Jeff smiled. "I must really mean something to you. Otherwise you wouldn't be afraid."

"Don't flatter yourself." Stepping forward, Meredith placed her arms around his neck and slowly brought his face toward hers. Their lips touched and Jeff coaxed her mouth open with a probing insistence that made her knees feel weak. As his lips moved to her throat and neck, Meredith felt a passion surge through her like a bolt of lightning. Matching his intensity, she returned his caresses and pressed closer against him. She felt the overpowering need to be possessed...

Dear Reader:

We've had thousands of wonderful surprises at SECOND CHANCE AT LOVE since we launched the line in June 1981.

We knew we were going to have to work hard to bring you the six best romances we could each month. We knew we were working with a talented, caring group of authors. But we *didn't* know we were going to receive such a warm and generous response from readers. So the thousands of wonderful surprises are in the form of letters from readers like you who've been kind with your praise, constructive and helpful with your suggestions. We read each letter...and take it seriously.

It's been a thrill to ''meet'' our readers, to discover that the people who read SECOND CHANCE AT LOVE novels and write to us about them are so remarkable. Our romances can only get better and better as we learn more and more about you, the reader, and what you like to read.

So, I hope you will continue to enjoy SECOND CHANCE AT LOVE and, if you haven't written to us before, please feel free to do so. If you have written, keep in touch.

With every good wish,

SECOND CHANCE AT LOVE Staff
The Berkley/Jove Publishing Group
200 Madison Avenue
New York, New York 10016

# Second Chance at Love

## TOO NEAR THE SUN
# AIMEE DUVALL

## A
**SECOND CHANCE AT LOVE
BOOK**

To Pete and Peggy Chauvet:
for supporting me,
in spite of me.

## - 1 -

"OF ALL DAYS to be running late!" Meredith muttered.
Project Scorpio was the biggest assignment she'd ever
been given, and she was off to a bad start. Stopping
her rented car at the entrance to the base, she handed
her credentials to the guard. Her fingers drummed
impatiently on the steering wheel as she waited for
the checks and verifications to be done.

Knowing how much stock military men place on
promptness, she carefully rehearsed a little speech in
her mind. In all honesty, it hadn't been her fault.
She'd left Carmel at dawn, piloting the company's
small twin-engine aircraft, but she'd had to fight
strong head winds all the way, and the flight had taken
almost twice as long as it should have. Further, another executive of Aero-Dynamics was here in San
Diego and needed the plane later in the day. She'd
had to land at the commercial airport, all the way
across town, rather than on the strip right here on the
base. And the morning rush-hour traffic had been

horrendous. . . . But how receptive would Commander Ryan be to excuses? She knew so little about him! What she had managed to discover, however, had made her very curious.

She looked forward to meeting him. Not that she would be affected in the least by his reputed charms. Her experiences with Mark had taught her it didn't pay to trust a charming man. As her thoughts drifted to him, a trace of bitterness surfaced at the back of her throat. Would it ever stop hurting? Mark had worked at Aero-Dynamics for only a year, but in that time he had swept her completely off her feet. Then had come the shock of discovering she hadn't known him at all! Mark hadn't even mentioned he'd applied for a position with a Canadian firm, much less that his acceptance would mean the end of their relationship. The price for a few months of happiness had been too great.

The guard's approach startled her back to the present. Returning her papers, he waved her through the gate. Meredith pressed on the accelerator, fighting the urge to floor it, and drove into a large fenced area. She parked alongside a row of other vehicles and walked across an open section. A few feet from the hangar she stopped, took a deep breath, and then went inside.

The concrete floors sported large pools of water and oil that she had to skirt carefully as she walked to the office area. Her long blonde hair bounced around her shoulders. Her navy blue jumpsuit accentuated her statuesque hourglass figure. Ignoring the many looks from the mechanics and flight technicians, Meredith pulled the door open and entered. The reception room was empty. Forty-five minutes late as it was, she invited herself upstairs.

Doors stood ajar on the second floor, but each

office she peered into was empty. There were the encouraging sounds of clacking typewriters and voices, though, and she dashed across the hall to slip through a partially open door. Immediately the dull gray lockers all around and—worse—the ping and hiss of hard-sprayed water signaled her obvious mistake. Meredith froze to the spot.

"Who the hell are you?"

Instinctively Meredith whirled toward the voice, which boomed from a shower stall across the room. There was no curtain, and she started at the sight of one of the most beautiful male bodies she'd ever seen . . . or dreamed of seeing! Her eyes locked on the massive chest where curling dark hair glistened with water, and refused to move upward to meet his.

"Well, at least hand me a towel."

"I, uh, oh, Lord!" Meredith grabbed a towel from the stack on the bench to her right. In one quick motion, she tossed it and turned, then dashed back out into the hallway, slamming the door behind her.

The noise brought a tall fair-haired man into the corridor. He looked hard at her for a moment, and then began to laugh. Struggling to compose herself, Meredith swallowed convulsively.

"I . . ." She paused to clear her voice, then continued, trying to sound more confident. "I have a meeting with Commander Ryan. I'm already very late, so if you can just tell me where I can find him, I'd appreciate it."

"Are you Meredith Buchanan?"

"I am."

"I hate to tell you this, but that meeting is over. It let out about fifteen minutes ago. To answer your second question, I think you've already had the pleasure of meeting Commander Ryan."

Meredith extended her hand. "I'm sorry, sir. I realize I'm extremely late, but—"

"Hold it! I'm not the commander. He's the one in the shower."

Her cheeks burned as she smiled stiffly. "Should have known from your insignia, of course."

"But not mine?" a voice behind her questioned suggestively.

"Oh, no!" she muttered softly. She hadn't heard the door to the locker room open.

"Well, now, who is our sightseer here?"

There was challenge in that voice, and Meredith turned around abruptly. Commander Ryan's blue eyes had a curious penetrating quality. His face, as handsome to Meredith as his physique had been impressive, was framed by wavy black hair sprinkled with just a touch of gray at the temples. He had about him an indefinable look of authority and assurance that announced: here's a man used to giving orders and having them followed.

"Commander, this is Meredith Buchanan," The fair-haired man said quickly.

"You certainly know how to make an entrance!" He shook his head, then went on. "By the way, we were expecting your company's chief engineer to personally oversee the testing. Instead, they've sent us his assistant. Why?"

Meredith bristled. "I'm no mere assistant. I've been on this project since the beginning. I helped design the Scorpio as well as supervise the construction of the prototype. I know that aircraft like I know the palm of my hand. When our chief was called away on business, it was logical that I should be put in charge. I assure you my engineering credentials are excellent, Commander. Otherwise, Aero-Dynamics would have never given me full control."

"You do *not* have full control, Ms. Buchanan." The commander's mouth curled into a tight smile.

"Your job is to work with our engineers as well as out test pilots and implement any design changes we feel are necessary."

"I realize that, Commander. I only meant—"

"It doesn't matter what you *meant*. Also, in the future I expect you to arrive promptly for all briefings. I won't tolerate tardiness."

Meredith's eyes flared, but before she had a chance to reply he nodded curtly, turned on his heel and strided briskly down the hall.

"Of all the nerve!"

"Ms. Buchanan, I think you've got that reversed. I mean you *are* incredibly late, and you did . . . er, *intrude* on his shower!"

"Where are the others who attended the meeting? I need to find out what was discussed," Meredith snapped.

"I was at the meeting. I'll be glad to fill you in."

"You know who I am, but I don't know who you are. Would you mind correcting that?"

The officer extended his hand. "My name is Allan Webber. I'm the executive officer."

Accepting his hand, Meredith relented and smiled. "Okay, I'll admit I blew it. Why don't you give me the essentials, just so I'll know exactly what went down and where they want to begin work. By the way, what do I call you, lieutenant commander *and* executive officer?"

"Allan will do just fine." He grinned.

"Got it. Call me Meredith."

They stepped into a small office across the way, where Allan briefed her on the meeting. The tests of the Scorpio would start the following afternoon. She'd been assigned a work area on that floor and would be given any assistance she needed for helping to evaluate and analyze performance data.

"For now, however, I think you better get to know

our facilities," he said. Meredith rose, signaling her agreement. "How about if I give you the guided tour now?" She nodded and followed him into the corridor. He smiled. "Directly across is the pilots' locker room, but you've already seen that."

"Rub it in, mister. That's all I need," Meredith shot back.

Allan winked and led the way down the hall. "This will be your office for the duration of the project."

The room, although far from spacious, was adequately supplied with the necessary equipment. Her desk, directly in front of a large window, was metal and painted in the same dull gray color of everything else in the building. The room radiated all the warmth and charm of a monk's cell.

"Thank you," Meredith replied, looking around. "Right now, however, I'd like to go and check on the prototype, if you don't mind. I want to verify that everything is where it should be and in working order. By the way, who's going to take her up?"

"Commander Ryan."

"In that case, I want to spend *all* the time between now and then with the aircraft!" she said tartly.

"If you need access to our computers . . ."

"No, I have a portable terminal out in the car. It links up with our computer facilities in Carmel. I'll go get it, along with some of the specifications I need. I should get right to work. If you have any kind of table I can set up in the general vicinity of the aircraft, I'd sure appreciate it."

"Consider it done."

Meredith walked to her car, retrieved her things, then returned. The fighter prototype was parked at a corner of the hangar, and already a table and a chair had been placed by its side. A man dressed in overalls was standing by it, waiting.

"Hello," Meredith said.

"Ms. Buchanan, your office is on the line. You can take it over there," he said, pointing to a telephone on the wall.

Meredith thanked him and strode toward it, then picked up the receiver. "Meredith Buchanan. What can I do for you?"

"Hi! This is Bea." The administrative assistant at Aero-Dynamics had over the years become her closest friend. "Sorry to bother you, hon, but I've got a priority request from the top."

"Rats! I'm swamped. I've got enough work here for two people. What do they want me to do?"

"We need you to go to the west side of the base and report to a Captain Rawlings. The terrain-following radar of an A-12 has to be tested."

"There's no way I can do it before tonight without getting behind on the Scorpio, which is supposed to be tested tomorrow. Which has priority?"

"The Scorpio. Do the other when you can. However, get in touch with the captain as soon as possible. He's waiting for your call."

"Okay."

"If you have any questions, you're to call Hans Christie here at our office. He's the one who's taken care of the project until now."

"All right. I'll take care of it right away."

"Good. Meredith," Bea said in a lilting voice, "you know I'm jealous as anything?"

"Jealous?"

"Of you. Down there with all those gorgeous daredevils in uniform!"

"You're incorrigible," Meredith chided, laughing, and then Bea clicked off. Meredith dialed the base operator and was put through to Captain Rawlings.

"Hello, Ms. Buchanan," he said. "I've been expecting your call, and I'll get right to the point. The Lab has calibrated the terrain-following the radar for automatic flight at 200 feet from the surface. Now we need to flight-test it."

"I'm afraid Scorpio has priority, so I won't be able to get away until this evening. Do you have any objections to conducting the flight after dinner time?"

The captain paused. "Well, it'll have to do, won't it?"

"We could schedule it for the day after tomorrow."

"No. I want this done as soon as possible. I won't be able to take you up, so I'll have one of my men standing by for you. Do you expect any problems?"

"None, sir. Actually it's a very simple process. All I need is someone who is familiar with the aircraft."

"In that case, we'll expect you at seven."

"Where shall I meet with your man?"

"Come to the west side of the base. We're across from the research lab and about a mile from the control tower. He'll be waiting for you."

"His name?"

"Depending on who I can get, it will either be Lieutenant Dailey or Lieutenant Commander Hart."

"All right. I'll be there."

Meredith sighed and returned to the Scorpio. Skipping lunch, she rushed to finish her checks before quitting time. She was starving by then, and the last thing she wanted was food from a military mess! She drove to a restaurant a few miles outside the base, which she'd spotted on her way in this morning, and ordered a mammoth dinner. The waitress ogled Meredith's trim figure as she removed the dishes that no longer bore a single trace of chicken-fried steak, mashed potatoes, gravy, and salad.

The weather had changed for the worse. The distant rumble of thunder accompanied her on her drive back to base, then rain pelted her as she left her car and made for the hangar, cursing her luck. It was too bad the A-12 was an *all*-weather attack aircraft, otherwise there might have been hope for a cancellation.

In the ladies' room at the hangar she changed quickly, then shoved the papers she needed for the radar check into a zippered pocket located over her right thigh. Although the flight suit was literally covered with zippered pockets, that one was the handiest. Carrying a small waterproof bag of tools she'd brought from the car, she made for the plane.

Attack planes always look the same, she thought. Barrel shaped with short swept-back wings, they exhibit none of the sleekness found in the fighters. Although perfectly suited for their function, able to sustain plenty of battle damage without being incapacitated, they were not her favorite aircraft. Yet there was something to be said for the tough and scrappy planes. It was easy to see why the crews had named this one the Bulldog. Despite its ugliness it had a certain charm.

Meredith climbed aboard. Waving away an offer of help from the plane's captain, she strapped herself in and checked her parachute. The pilot introduced himself as Rick Dailey. She murmured an acknowledgment, then nodded at a crew man who hooked up her oxygen and G suit. Leaving her side, he finished helping the pilot, then jumped to the ground.

"Ready?" came the voice from the front seat.

"Ready."

They were towed out of the hangar by a small yellow tractor. As the tow cable was loosened, the plane captain stood by the side of the aircraft, well in the pilot's view. Meredith felt the engines come alive. Glancing around, she searched for the access panel, then spotted it to her right. Although she wanted to study it, the harness kept her locked in place. She grew impatient. She'd put in a full day and she wanted to get this over with. When the jets reached the proper levels, the pilot taxied out.

As the aircraft picked up speed, Meredith kept her eyes on the streak of concrete going past her window. The runway lights, dazzling in intensity and color, began to meld into one long, continuous line. As the pressure propelled her against the back of her seat, she felt the exhilaration of takeoff pulsing through her veins. The engines vibrating below her heaved and throbbed, matching the excitement she always felt at the beginning of a flight. In a matter of seconds, the aircraft lifted its nose and shot into the night sky. It was no small wonder pilots so loved their jobs!

"It'll be a short trip," came the pilot's voice over her earphones. "We'll be heading toward the water, then I'll drop the altitude so you can do your thing."

"Good enough."

Meredith saw lightning flash across the darkened skies, but paid little heed. Although she was no great fan of electrical storms, the aircraft had been built to withstand them. With a competent pilot at the controls, there was little to do but wait until her turn came to do her work.

"Not much of a flight, is it?" the pilot asked rhetorically.

"If you mean the view, you're right. It stinks."

"We'll be over water in another ten minutes. Anything special you want me to do?"

"Sure," she said. "Hold her as steady as you can while I work."

"Can do."

Meredith glanced around her. The soft glow inside the cockpit seemed blinding in comparison to the endless expanse of blackness around the plane. When the aircraft began to descend, she realized they had reached the ocean. The water below was lost in the darkness as they skimmed across its surface at incredible speed. Feeling like someone trapped in a long dark tunnel, she shook her head and addressed herself to the task at hand. Removing the plate covering the access panel, she waited for Rick to level off.

"Okay. We're at 170 feet, a little lower than our optimum altitude. It'll be better for the automatic control to pull us up a bit rather than down. Let me know when you're ready."

Meredith unscrewed the bolt to the panel that held the mechanism at a set altitude. She watched the metal wheel turn slowly, after the pilot said "Switching to automatic now."

The aircraft climbed to 200 feet, then leveled off, maintaining the proper distance from the water. Over land, it would automatically compensate for changing terrain, allowing it to fly steadily at the 200 feet altitude at which it had been set.

"The altimeter checks out," the pilot confirmed.

"Good. I'll keep up the observation back here."

Concentrating, she kept her eyes fixed on the dial. Suddenly a brilliant flash illuminated the entire cockpit. Meredith rubbed her eyes in an attempt to clear her vision. "What was that?"

"Lightning," said the smooth voice from the front.

"You mean we just got hit?"

*"Rajah."*

Meredith shook her head. Maybe this was all old hat to him, but it certainly wasn't to her! What was she doing out here?

"I don't want to alarm you, but we may have a problem. There's a bit of white smoke coming from the control panel. Can you hear me all right?"

"Yes," Meredith said.

"Let me try the base. By the way, I'd like to head home as soon as you're through."

"Suits me. Give me a couple of seconds to verify my work and I'll be ready." While she worked, Meredith heard the pilot trying to contact the base.

*"Night Hawk One* to Pinpoint. Do you read me?"

There was silence after his call.

"Ms. Buchanan, I think our radio is putting out but just not receiving. I can't be sure. Are you ready?"

"Yes. Take her out of automatic. I'm more than ready to go home."

"Good deal."

Meredith waited, but nothing happened; the aircraft still flew at the same altitude.

"Bad news," the pilot said. "We're locked in automatic. I think the lightning messed up more than just the radio. Let me try again."

Meredith waited breathlessly for a sign all was normal, but none came. Instead of the slow ascent she hoped for, the aircraft continued flying straight and level.

"Can you reset the altitude as we fly?"

"No, not unless the autopilot is off. The altimeter is locked into place." Meredith paused, then added, "However, I can get to the controls from back here. Let me see what I can do."

"All right. If I can be of help, holler."

"You got it."

*"Night Hawk One* calling Pinpoint," the pilot said calmly into the transmitter. "We have sustained some damage to our controls. Aircraft is locked on autopilot. We are attempting to correct. I'm sending this message blind, hoping you can pick it up. Communications may be impaired. I'm flying on course 225 back to base. Estimated distance, eighty miles. Out."

Meredith concentrated on the panel at her side. Unscrewing two top bolts, she swung the panel down and out of the way. Inside, the maze of wires seemed to be greater than she had remembered. Seeing a couple of heavily armored cables, she smiled. "I've got them," she said. "There's only one problem. One cable is for the automatic, the other is for manual controls. I've got no way of telling which is which."

"I can't help you there."

"I'm going to try and nip away at this outer covering. Wouldn't you know it. It's covered with braided aluminium. I don't want to damage my wire cutters, so it might be a while. I'll let you know when I get inside."

"Look, I'm keeping the transmitter on. If anyone is listening, they'll at least know what we're doing."

"Good idea."

Meredith whittled away at the exterior. Minutes ticked by as she methodically pried bits and pieces off the cable. Digging, she felt the covering give way, exposing several red and black wires. "Got it. I'm going to cut through."

"Wait. I'll put her into a turn. She'll climb a few feet that way. If we dip any, at least we'll have a little more altitude to maneuver with."

"You say the word."

As the aircraft went into a shallow turn, he ordered, "Now!"

Meredith cut through the wires. The aircraft climbed for a few seconds, then resumed the locked-in altitude. Resisting the urge to curse loudly, she closed her eyes for a few seconds.

"No go. Wrong cable. Better cut the other one," the pilot said.

"Okay, then I'll go to the other side. Unless we cut the auto-control wires on both sides, it won't do any good. This aircraft is built with redundant systems."

"Remember, though, if you cut the wrong cable on the other side, we won't have any controls at all."

"No problem, now that I know which is which."

Meredith slowly pried away the outer covering, then, forcing the wire cutters with both hands, snipped through the second cable. "What's our fuel status?" she asked.

"Not good. You've got less than five minutes to get everything done. Otherwise, we won't have enough fuel to make it all the way back."

"Hang on. I have no intention of swimming home. I'll get it done on time," Meredith said.

"I hate to bring this up, but a thought just occurred to me. What if they've placed the cables in opposite order on that panel to ensure survivability of the system in case of battle damage?"

"Oh, good. I really needed that." She remained silent as she opened the second panel. "Here they are."

"What are you going to do?"

"Punt," she muttered.

"What was that?"

"I believe they'd keep these cables in the same order. Think about it. What are the chances a round would pass exactly straight through the aircraft? And a reversed arrangement would drive the maintenance people nuts!"

"Good point. Are you ready for me to start going into a turn?"

"No," she said. "I've still got to pry off the armor before I can get to the wires."

"We have about three minutes."

"I don't need a running count," she said lightly as she snipped away at the covering, trying to control a slight tremor in her hands. It could be the wrong cable. If it was, they would probably flip over into the water. Perspiration dripped freely inside her flight suit. She worked frantically.

"How's it coming?"

"So-so. If I damage these wire cutters, I won't be able to cut the cable at all. Take a deep breath, and if you feel like praying, don't let me stop you."

"You've got one minute."

"I don't want to know," she protested. With a final

effort, the cutters broke through the covering and exposed the wires. "I have it!" she crowed.

"If it's the right cable."

"You're a regular ray of sunshine, you know that?"

"I'm starting the turn. Cut on my signal." There was a pause. "Now!" he ordered.

Meredith cut the cable. Slowly the nose edged upward, the plane climbing steadily into the night sky.

"That's the way!" he yelled into the speaker.

"Taxi driver, take me home!"

"You got it, lady!"

Meredith prayed silently that no more mishaps would plague the already damaged aircraft. Wind turbulence tossed them as they sped toward the base. Passing through a particularly rough air pocket, she felt her hands grow clammy. If she could only see something outside her window, things wouldn't be so bad. The void seemed to engulf them, sheathing them in a dreary blanket of darkness. Taking a deep breath, she tried to remain calm. As she struggled to catch a glimpse of civilization, she spotted the runway lights directly ahead.

Lining up, the pilot began a steady descent. Mesmerized by the twinkle of lights framing the runway, Meredith smiled. They had made it! Feeling the landing gear lock into place, she leaned back, anticipating their touchdown. When the wheels met the runway, she felt the familiar jolt.

"Don't look now," the pilot warned, "but I think we've got a reception committee waiting for us!"

They taxied to a stop a few hundred yards from the tower, then climbed out of the cockpit and were greeted by the operations personnel, all rain soaked but sporting wide smiles. Captain Rawlings accompanied Commander Ryan onto the field. The two men escorted Meredith and the lieutenant back to the hangar.

"Damn good job, Dailey! Damn good!" Captain Rawlings declared.

Meredith shook her head in disbelief, then laughed. "Yes, Lieutenant Dailey. Thanks for getting us back."

Dailey blushed. "Actually, *she* was the one who saved the situation, sir. All I did was fly the aircraft."

The captain turned toward her. "Oh, yes, certainly. I didn't mean to belittle your contribution, Ms. Buchanan. Very good head you have on your shoulders."

Meredith bit her tongue to keep from laughing. "Good of you to notice, sir."

As Commander Ryan sauntered to her side, he whispered good-naturedly, "Don't mind him. You did an excellent job. Glad to have you both back in one piece."

Meredith nodded. "Thanks. Now, if you don't mind, I'd like to drive back to my hotel. There's lots of work to be done on the Scorpio tomorrow."

"Let me drive you back."

"No. I can manage. Good night, Commander."

"Look, I really—"

"Night!" she said, running toward her parked car.

# - 2 -

THE FOLLOWING MORNING Meredith worked fever-
ishly, trying to get the Scorpio in shape for the test
run. News of her flight spread quickly, and soon it
seemed everyone had heard about last night's adven-
ture. She noticed the men looking at her speculatively
from time to time, when they thought she wasn't
watching. As she double-checked all the panels, she
felt a hand touch her shoulder.

"Hi! Heard you had quite an evening," Allan commented.

"I don't want to even think about it! I've got to
keep my mind on this," she said, patting the aircraft
in front of her.

"How's it going?"

"I'm trying to check everything. I want to make
darn sure there are no surprises this afternoon."

"Is there anything you need, or any way I can
help?"

"No, but I really think it would be better to postpone the testing until tomorrow."

"Sorry. Our people have checked out the plane already, and they found nothing wrong. Unless you find something this morning, the test is on."

"Understood." Meredith turned her attention back to her work. She only had a few hours before the test. If they wouldn't postpone it, she had to make certain everything was in mint condition.

It seemed she had just started, when Allan sauntered back in. "Hey! It's time. We're going to tow the aircraft outside for Commander Ryan. Get whatever you need and come with me."

Meredith smirked. "You didn't give me enough time. I should really check the rest of the systems."

"Have you found anything wrong?"

"No, but that doesn't mean that everything's fine. I need at least another hour or so."

"Sorry. I've got my instructions."

Meredith followed him silently. Well, the Navy engineers had looked it over, and what she had been able to check was in good shape. She knew, however, that some of the systems could not be considered reliable until the aircraft was actually tested. The wind, pressure, and runway conditions would have their effects, bringing any bugs the Scorpio might have to the surface. It was part of her job to observe and determine the cause of a malfunction, but today the thought of Commander Ryan piloting the fighter bothered her. Well, she had a job to do, and he had his. There was no sense in letting any other worries crowd her mind. Yet, despite her efforts to counter it, something nagged at the back of her mind, and the tightening in her stomach persisted.

Standing by the side of the runway with several other engineers and technicians, Meredith saw the commander emerge from the hangar and walk confidently toward the Scorpio. Small recesses built into the fuselage allowed him to climb aboard, then ease himself into the cockpit. The black-and-red flight suit of his squadron, accentuated his massive shoulders and muscular build. Meredith watched as he strapped himself in with the aid of one of his plane captains. He adjusted his helmet, bringing the built-in oxygen mask to his face and locking the visor into place. Now he was ready. He started the engines and waited until the wail of the jets grew to a dull roar.

Sealing the canopy, he began a slow taxi down the runway. Meredith held her breath. There was a certain quality about him, something undefinable that made it impossible to forget he was a man. She scarcely knew him, yet she couldn't deny the very dangerous attraction she felt.

Without warning, the fighter, still moving at low speed, deviated from its path. With her stomach tied into a knot, Meredith watched it veer to one side and come to a stop, sliding into the mud on the left of the runway. There was an odd sucking sound as the flaps dug into the soft ground.

Within seconds the entire field was in motion. Meredith ran toward the aircarft, ignoring the mud. She stopped a few feet from the Scorpio.

"What the hell happened to this thing? It was doing fine, then the brakes locked and off to the side we went. Who was supposed to check her out?" Ryan demanded, his voice hard and impatient. Seeing Meredith approach, he looked down at her from the plane and gave her a lopsided grin. "We sure do meet in the oddest places!"

Meredith felt an incredible surge of relief. Seeing his eyes focus on the ground, she followed his gaze. Her stomach lurched as she realized she had sunk several inches into the dark-colored ooze. Instinctively yanking one of her feet free, Meredith lost her balance and fell.

"Pfui!" Slowly standing back up, she tried to clean

some of the oil and dirt from her face and clothing. As she glanced toward the cockpit, she saw Jeff grinning.

Her cheeks flashed tones of red like a colored neon sign. Her eyes blazed with fury as she tried to pry herself free and return to hard ground. "Don't say a word," she warned, her voice glacial enough to turn the Pacific into a large block of ice.

Jeff looked at her speculatively. Suddenly he climbed down from the cockpit and walked toward her. Other base personnel, busy with their tasks and knowing neither were in danger, continued to work on the trapped fighter, ignoring them completely.

"Come on. Let me help you out of here. God, you're a mess!"

"This is your fault, you abominable idiot!"

"My fault? Hell, I didn't push you into the mud!"

"If I hadn't been concerned that something had happened to..."

Meredith's eyes grew large; what was she saying? "uh... to the aircraft, I wouldn't have fallen."

"To the fighter, huh?" The smiling blue eyes mocked her. "Here I thought you were worried about me!"

"Don't flatter yourself. I've worked long and hard on the design of the Scorpio."

"You look lousy. Why don't you use my shower upstairs? I'll even be glad to toss you a towel."

Meredith's eyes bored into him. "You are insufferable!" Walking past him, she attempted a grand exit. The sound of squishing mud trapped inside her shoes robbed her of the hoped-for effect. She picked up her purse in the hangar and strode briskly to the parking lot.

She leaned against the side of her car and wiped the mud off her hands with a clean handkerchief. Dabbing her forehead and eyes, she suddenly felt a third hand touch her face. Startled, she took a step backward. Jeff stood in front of her, looking directly at her. There was something in his eyes, a peculiar but reassuring expression. She had no doubt he had carefully perfected it over the years to achieve just the effect he wanted.

"I don't need help, thank you."

"Where are you staying?" he demanded in his best commander's voice.

"The Four Winds," she heard herself reply before realizing her mistake.

"I'll pick you up at eight. We'll have dinner."

"Commander, I have no intention—"

"My name is Jeff. See you at eight." Leaving without giving her a chance to reply, he turned and headed back toward the mud-covered fighter and the crew around it.

"You can come whenever you want, bozo, but I'm not going anywhere with you!" she shouted. Opening her car door, she slid behind the wheel, then slammed the door shut with a vengeance. This had not been her day! She would go directly to the hotel, take the longest bath in recorded history, and go straight to bed.

Finding her way out of base proved simple, but Meredith cringed when she saw the reaction on the face of the guard at the gate. She had to look a perfect horror. Glancing at her soiled clothing, she shook her head in disgust. The mud had begun to dry in spots, caking and cracking.

Arriving at the hotel, Meredith locked the car and went inside. Feeling the stares, she kept her eyes straight ahead. A small child, unaware and unrestricted by the codes of the adults around him, pointed to her and laughed. Silently cursing the slowness of the elevator, Meredith tried to shut out everything around her. How could she have been stupid enough to walk right into the mud? Remembering Jeff's mocking eyes, Meredith felt her temper flare. He was such an insensitive clod! When the elevator doors slid open, she stepped inside and pressed her floor number.

The day had started off badly and gone downhill rapidly. As her mind wandered through the events, Meredith stifled a small giggle, then laughed out loud. Quickly entering her room and making for the bathroom, she looked at herself in the full-length mirror. What a sight she made! She laughed even harder and stripped off her mud-smeared clothes, letting her skirt and blouse fall to the tiled floor.

Remembering the time she had interrupted Jeff's shower, she smiled impishly. Too bad she hadn't looked even harder! But the memory of his offer to her of the use of that same shower—and the undeniable attraction she'd felt at his suggestive banter—unexpectedly brought Mark's betrayal to mind. No, never again would something like that happen to her. She would keep her guard up and not let physical needs lure her into a trap.

Once the tub was filled, Meredith gently lowered herself into the scalding water. Closing her eyes, she forced herself to relax. Confident in her abilities as an engineer, she knew that in time the others would see her worth. Her thoughts slowly drifted back to Jeff. She was *very* attracted to him. It was useless to deny it, but she would not let it interfere with work.

What would she do about tonight? She couldn't allow him to think he could simply order her to go out with him to dinner...yet there was a definite value in establishing a good rapport with the Scorpio's test pilot. His opinions and judgments would be the focal point of many modifications. If she was unable to work with him, the project could be jeopardized. Meredith struggled with her conscience, trying to come to an equitable solution. Stepping out of the tub, she dried off and sat on the bed. She had to make

Jeff see her as a professional and a person who was easy to get along with. Yes, she would have dinner with him. It was, after all, to her own advantage.

Opening the closet, she selected a flowing off-white Quiana cocktail dress and picked out the highest-heeled shoes she had brought. Although she was by no means short, Jeff seemed to tower over her, and with him she needed the height of those stiletto heels. She was determined to look her best tonight and to try to have fun. It was important, too, that she set things back on the right track. Tossing the garment over her head, she finished dressing, then walked toward the mirror. The dress shimmered under the light, giving her a soft look. Sitting in front of the vanity, she applied a bit of makeup, then stopped. She was trying to think of a way to fix her hair. Her shoulder-length blonde hair curled around the edges, framing her face in soft waves. Brushing it vigorously, she worked slowly until wispy curls framed the sides of her face and the rest was swept neatly into a stylish French knot. Standing back, she assessed her appearance.

Not bad. Turning casually, letting the skirt float around her, she smiled at the image the mirror presented. She loved to dress up. She enjoyed the furtive glances and appraising looks others would bestow on her. It always helped pick up her spirits when she was feeling low.

He was late. When five minutes more had elapsed, she picked up her purse and coat, then left the room. She was locking her door when she heard Jeff's voice behind her.

"What's this? Were you going to start without me?"

Expecting an apology for his tardiness and not getting one, Meredith found her anger surge. "You said eight. It's eight-fifteen. I'm hungry and dislike waiting."

"I guess we're even. At least I didn't invite myself into your shower," he said, a roguish glint in his eye.

Meredith began to snap back an answer but then, controlling her fiery temper, smiled. "We're off to a very bad start," she said softly. "We're going to have to work together for quite a few weeks. It would be much more pleasant if we could at least be civilized around one another, you know."

"My thoughts exactly. Let me buy you a nice dinner, we'll share some wine, then I'll take you to see San Diego. Have you ever been here before?"

"No. One time I flew in late at night, then flew out the next morning, but that hardly counts."

"In that case, you'll have to let me show you around."

"I would be honored, Commander," Meredith replied with a grin.

"Forget Commander Ryan. He's back on the base. Tonight I'm Jeff. In fact, to you, I'm always Jeff."

She ignored that tacked-on sentence and asked brightly, "All right, Jeff, where to?" They stepped out of the elevator. Quickly crossing the parking lot, he stopped by the side of a silver Porsche and opened the door for her. Meredith, pleased by his manners, smiled. "Thank you."

Jeff slipped behind the wheel. "I'm going to take you to Harbor Island. My favorite restaurant is quite a place. It's right on the bay. You can hear the water rushing below you. It always is a comforting sound. It makes it easy to relax—at least it does for me."

"I know what you mean. I love the ocean and the marinas. There's a familiar atmosphere—the same kind of freedom I feel whenever I'm piloting the Cessna."

"You fly?"

"Yes, certainly. With my job, sometimes it isn't enough to have someone else describe a malfunction.

It's much better to get a firsthand experience."

"Oh, God!" he said in a horrified tone. "You don't mean you test the aircraft at your center?"

"Sure. Well, rarely, though. It's just sometimes pilots tend to blame an aircraft for their own mistakes. If I feel it's pilot error and they disagree, I like to judge for myself."

"Well, I assure you, I've been in this business for years, and when I say something is wrong, something is very definitely wrong."

"It's okay. I'm not trying to take your job from you. Besides, how did we ever get on this anyway?"

As they walked into the restaurant, Meredith noticed the defensiveness and tension in him. Trying not to let the evening go to hell, and determined to learn how to get along with him, she decided to let Jeff take control and lead the conversation to whatever areas he felt at ease with. She would watch him and learn his likes and dislikes.

Once they were seated, he seemed to relax. The restaurant was undeniably elegant. Huge windows lined the entire wall facing the bay. Decorated in dark wooden hues, it seemed to float on the water's edge. Conscious of the silence between them, Meredith looked up and smiled.

"Let's not talk shop," he said. "You know, you look absolutely beautiful."

Meredith averted her eyes. The standard line had still evoked a strange but pleasing sensation inside her. He was so damned good-looking! And so damned sexy. And, despite her resolutions, she found it impossible to ignore his magnetic appeal.

As they made small talk, her heart began to pound. He seemed to caress her with his every word . . . and his eyes. They drifted from her face, lingered on her throat, then dropped to her breasts. What would it be like to be held and kissed by him? Her nipples grew taut under his frankly admiring gaze as a feeling of total sensuality enveloped her.

She sought for a way to break the spell and, glancing down at his hands, had it. . . . He wore a ring of antique gold in the form of a shield. "What an unusual ring!" she exclaimed.

"It's my family's crest. The ring belonged to my father. When he passed away, I inherited it. It's been in my family for generations."

Almost casually he reached out, seizing her hand and cradling it between his two warm palms. Meredith felt the firmness of his grip. Not wanting to take her hand away, she waited.

"I noticed your ring, too," he commented, eyes on the intricately shaped coral stone in its center.

The small intaglio goddess had been meticulously hand carved. The ring had been made especially to her specifications in Honolulu, and Meredith was proud of it.

"The goddess's name is Etoine, hell's dark mistress," she murmured. She wasn't about to mention that the goddess was supposed to empower her followers with the ability to use deceit to further their own ends, without ever falling prey to it. Nor was she even tempted to tell him she had bought it as a reminder of her past and the mistakes she would never again repeat. With a mysterious smile, she remained quiet.

"All right, you don't have to tell me more about it. But you must admit it's rather unusual."

"Yes, it is."

When the waiter approached their table, Jeff released her hand. Still feeling the warmth of his touch, she tried to concentrate on the varied selection of food the restaurant offered. She glanced up at him, then on an impulse closed the menu and set it by the side of the table.

"You order for me."

"I don't know what you like..."

"Oh, I think you do..." she said softly.

Jeff smiled.

"Will you have cocktails before dinner?" the waiter asked.

"Meredith?"

"I'd like a glass of cream sherry, please."

"A glass of cream sherry for my lady, and a Scotch and water for me."

Meredith didn't fail to pick up that "my," but decided not to appear to notice. She would have to learn to let go and have a bit more fun. Surely Jeff posed no real threat to her. She was attracted to him, but why not enjoy the attraction? If he enjoyed this type of game, what harm?

After a few minutes the waiter brought their drinks. "Are you ready to order now?"

"Yes. First we'll have beef consommé, then lobster."

"Dressing on the salads?"

"Yes, blue cheese," he responded, looking directly at Meredith for confirmation.

Meredith nodded.

As soon as the waiter left, she picked up her glass. "Shall we toast?"

"All right. What would you like to toast to?"

"How about to new friendships?" As Meredith sipped her drink, Jeff's eyes locked with hers. His look held such a penetrating intensity, she was certain he had just memorized her every feature. Glancing away, she gazed at the ocean.

"You're right. This is a lovely restaurant." Candles at the center of the table shimmered softly, adding a glow to their surroundings, while music played quietly in the background. Outside, the lights of the harbor played upon the water, glittering and sparkling upon the surface. The mood was one of relaxation, and soon she felt the tensions of the day completely recede to the back of her mind.

"I haven't felt this comfortable with anyone since..." Suddenly aware she had said too much, Meredith's eyes widened slightly as she fiddled with the napkin on her lap.

"Since when?"

"Long time ago."

The waiter brought their first course. Meredith was ravenous. Looking up occasionally as she savored the rich consommé, she wondered at the way he measured and studied her reactions.

"Well, are you pleased?" he asked.

"Yes, and the food is good, too."

Jeff laughed and reached for her hand. Immediately aware of the firmness of his grip, Meredith found herself enjoying the way his finger caressed the back of her hand.

"Your skin is very soft."

"Not what you expected in the hands of an engineer?" she said teasingly.

He stroked her palm. "Can't remember ever being interested in any part of an engineer's body before— except his brain," Jeff said huskily.

Meredith was breathing raggedly, a dangerous excitement rippling through her. "How did you get to be a test pilot?" she asked in a hoarse voice.

"I joined the Navy right after college." His eyes twinkled with the knowledge of her diversionary tactic. After a long pause, Meredith had the odd sensation he was telling her silently he'd let her get by with it—*this time!* "I always knew I wanted to fly fighter aircraft," he continued, "and when the opportunity to test new models came my way, I just couldn't resist the challenge."

"Do you still enjoy it as much today as when you began?"

"There's nothing in the world like it, Meredith. Every day is different."

"Different, too, in the dangers. . . . A really good pilot knows instinctively how far he can push his aircraft. Besides, there's a series of checks and balances as you well know. If things get really heavy, I can always eject."

They chatted amiably about themselves throughout the rest of the meal. But with coffee, Jeff reverted to his previous flirtatious manner. The gentleness in him stirred forgotten emotions buried deep within Meredith, and she was glad when he suddenly turned his attention to the door. Following his glance, she saw a beautiful, tall, raven-haired woman staring directly at them.

"Wait here, I'll be right back."

"Is there a problem?" Meredith asked tartly.

Reaching for her hand and squeezing it reassuringly, he shook his head. "I'll be right back."

Meredith saw him walk toward the woman, then they both disappeared from view. Incredibly curious, she decided this was a good time to powder her nose. She got up and headed in their direction, with the pretense of looking for the ladies' restroom. As she neared the lobby, she could see them talking by the door. Edging closer, she stepped into a recess by the wall and listened.

"I waited for you to call. I never even left the house, Jeff. You said you'd call within the week. Two weeks have gone by and I haven't heard a word. I thought you really cared, and now I find you here with that little bitch."

"Lower your voice, Margot. Let's get right to the point. There was never anything between us. You liked me, I liked you, and for awhile it was good with us. For God's sake, I didn't want to force a confrontation! Couldn't you get the hint when I didn't call you back? What in the hell is the matter with you?"

Meredith, hearing the frigid edge in his voice, shuddered. It brought back memories of her final meeting with Mark so many months ago. She knew exactly the humiliation and hurt felt by the woman he so callously rejected. Not wanting to hear any more, she returned to their table.

How could she have imagined even fleetingly that Jeff might be different? If he could be so cruel and insensitive to a woman he obviously had shared a relationship with, what could she expect from him? Shaking her head, she grew fiercely determined. She would use him, before he had a chance to hurt her. She would need his cooperation to successfully complete her job, but she would never allow him to get to her emotionally. She would never forget the scene in the lobby, no matter how convincing or sincere he seemed to her.

Within a few minutes, Jeff returned. With the same caressing quality he had for her in his voice before, he apologized for his absence. "There's dancing in the next room," he said. "Shall we?"

"No, I think not." The idea of settling inside his strong arms to dance disturbed her. His physical magnetism was so undeniable she had to maintain a guard.

When they finished their coffee, he pushed back his chair, then came around to assist her.

"Thank you for dinner, Jeff. It was lovely."

"The evening isn't over yet. I want to take you to my favorite place. I think you'll enjoy it."

"Where?"

"You'll see."

Meredith found herself hard pressed to keep up with him as they cut across the lobby and to the parking lot. "Whoa! I'm not much of a jogger, you know," she said.

Looking contrite, he slowed his pace. "You should have told me. I'm used to walking fast. I didn't mean to get you out of breath."

"Okay. It's just that your strides are much longer than mine. It's all right now. I can keep up with you at this speed."

Jeff almost carelessly placed his arm around her shoulders, and Meredith, annoyed, dropped her small evening bag. He immediately bent over to retrieve it for her. When he handed it back, she gracefully accepted it and moved casually away from his reach. Not bad, she thought, trying to suppress a grin. That ploy never failed to work.

Jeff drove too fast, and Meredith was relieved when he slowed down and parked at an overlook illuminated only by the stars and the nearly full moon. The scene was breathtakingly beautiful. Pounding waves beat against the rocky cliffs; in pools between boulders the foam-laced water eddied violently.

"Gorgeous!" she exclaimed—and exciting, she thought.

Jeff moved alongside her and reached for her hand. "It's called Shadow Cliffs. Here San Diego Bay meets the Pacific Ocean."

Meredith inhaled deeply, allowing the salty sea air to fill her nostrils. Suddenly, as if awakening from a dream, she felt Jeff move up close behind her. Every nerve in her body tensed. As the warmth of his breath touched the nape of her neck, she spun around abruptly, intending to put a stop to whatever he had in mind. Immediately she began to speak, but Jeff's mouth came down on hers, smothering her protest.

Meredith tried to push him back, but his arms held her steady while his mouth moved against hers. His lips were firm but gentle as they brushed tantalizingly

over hers, coaxing...coaxing...coaxing them to
part. The tenderness of his approach was undoing her.
Her senses began to swim and, as his hands began to
run slowly up and down her sides, her breathing grew
shallow and labored. Swept with sudden weakness,
she melted against his muscular body. His arms tightened around her, his hands hotly possessive on her
back.

"So beautiful," he muttered against her open
mouth. "Oh, Meredith..."

Their kiss deepened, growing urgent. Meredith's
arms wrapped around his waist and locked his body
against hers. They swayed rhythmically as their
mouths clung, tongues meeting in searching hunger.
He drew back, cupped her face in his hands, and
gazed deep and questioningly into her eyes. There
was such passionate intensity in those blue depths that
Meredith shuddered. She wanted to answer yes to at
least one of his unspoken questions by pressing her
body hard against his. She resisted the violent urge
and, instead, held herself away, returning his penetrating stare. Bathed in moonlight, the tang of sea in
her nostrils and the pounding surf filling her ears,
Meredith was mesmerized by Jeff's eyes, their promise of ecstasy and more...much more. He was com-
municating a great deal about himself, beyond his
qualities as a lover. She saw a strong character, her
equal, a humorous personality, her match, a man who
could get under her skin, really matter to her. She
was flooded with sudden terror and tore herself free
in one desperate effort.

Eyes narrowed, he watched her pace in front of
him. "Tell me you enjoyed that as much as I did,"
he ordered in a low, husky voice.

"I'm not one of your subordinates, *Commander!*"

"Stop it," he snarled. "Don't degrade yourself by
denying the truth...and that fierceness in your voice

tries to do just that, my dear!"

"Truth?" she said sarcastically. "Maybe the truth is that you've got to believe you're irresistible to women."

"Knock it off. You felt as passionate as I did. For a moment there I *was* irresistible to you and you know it!"

"My, my. Confident, aren't we?"

"You fool," he snorted in disgust and then spun on his heel, striding rapidly to the car.

When Meredith reached the automobile, Jeff was already inside and the engine was running. Letting herself in, she sat in stony silence. He was right and she knew it. But she also knew she was playing out of her league; Jeff Ryan was a very dangerous man. She had done the right thing, pushing him away, denying her hunger for him. He was too sure of himself and too self-centered. After Mark, this type of man was the last thing she wanted in her life. Maybe her words might put a small dent in Jeff's self-confidence with her and keep him at bay.

Arriving at the hotel, Jeff parked by the entrance. Not giving him a chance to get out of the car, Meredith grabbed her evening bag, slammed the car door shut, and stormed inside the lobby. Turning briefly, she caught a glimpse of the little sports car speeding off.

Meredith walked slowly to her room. A horrible end to a dreadful day. Well, she should have known better. Why was it she felt a twinge of sad regret? No matter, she told herself furiously, there would be plenty of work during the testing to keep her busy—and help her resist the arrogant, sexy Commander Jeff Ryan.

# - 3 -

FOR THE NEXT few weeks, Jeff hardly spoke to her. The times when their work dictated mutual coopera- tion, they both behaved with icy politeness and frigid efficiency.

Several aircraft problems were corrected, but two new test pilots had just been transferred to their proj- ect. Meredith called for a meeting to brief them. They would have to learn to work under her guidance. If Jeff was any indication of the type of men they would be, things were bound to get worse.

Arriving at the conference room, Meredith set up her slide projector and pinned a diagram to the board. She wanted to show them exactly what the problems with the Scorpio were and what steps had been taken to correct them. With a few minutes to spare, she turned off the lights and previewed some of the slides. Assuring herself all was in order, she moved to turn the lights on, but the sound of Jeff's voice stopped her.

"Oh, sure, she's absolutely beautiful, a real knock-out to look at. But believe me, one touch from her and you're guaranteed frostbite."

Meredith felt her skin prickle. How dare he discuss her in those terms! Hearing the response from his companion, however, she had to stifle a laugh.

"That sure sounds like sour grapes, Jeff. What happened, she the rare one who turned you down?"

Switching the lights on, Meredith stepped into the doorway and smiled pleasantly at the three men.

"Ms. Buchanan," Jeff drawled. "I'd like you to meet Mike Lockwood and Bill Huntley."

"Hi! I'm glad to meet you both," Meredith said, extending her hand.

"Our pleasure," Huntley responded.

"Now, what shall I call you? Lieutenant commander?"

"You can call me Bill, and just call him by his nickname," the pilot quipped.

Meredith turned toward Mike, waiting for his reply. Instead, she was surprised to see him turning positively crimson. He gave his companion a look meant to melt cold steel.

Meredith, a little hesitant but by now very curious, looked at him. Keeping her voice soft, she asked, "What is your nickname?"

"Mag . . . A . . ."

"I'm sorry, I just didn't catch that."

Bill, somewhere behind Meredith, snickered loudly; Jeff had turned to face the opposite side of the room and his shoulders shook visibly.

"Magnet Ass!" Mike virtually shouted.

"That's a very unusual nickname," Meredith said, trying to suppress a smile. "How did you get it?"

"I was shot down over Vietnam a couple of times," he mumbled.

Seeing his obvious discomfort, she decided to drop the subject and walked to the blackboard.

"As Commander Ryan knows, there was a problem with the Scorpio brakes. On one side they locked when the retaining pins slipped out of place, causing him to lose steering and inbed the aircraft in the mud."

"And I thought you had checked it all out that time," he retorted, with a malicious glint in his eyes.

"First, there hadn't been enough time to check out *all* the systems, and, second, the whole purpose of your job is to discover the deficiencies in the proto-type. We wouldn't want your job to become obsolete now, would we?"

"Fat chance."

Ignoring this remark, Meredith turned her attention to the other two men. Patiently explaining the next phase of testing, she tried to avoid Jeff's eyes, which she knew were lingering on her body. Whenever she did glance at him, he was looking at her hips or mouth or breasts, making her acutely uncomfortable. She felt hot and naked under his careful scrutiny. What power did he have that continued to excite her and draw her to him? Even now, when he was deliberately and rudely being provocative. He'd do anything to disrupt her concentration so she'd slip up and appear incompetent! She seethed. Rather curtly, she informed the two new pilots their aircraft would be arriving later that day.

"Great, I'm eager to find out how good this fighter really is!" came the response from Bill.

"We will be working and testing three versions of the Scorpio simultaneously. That way we'll save time and money."

After a few more minutes, the meeting ended and the two new pilots promptly left the conference room. Jeff just sat still, though, waiting as Meredith made a few notes.

"Yes, Commander. Do you have a question?"

"Meredith, let's stop this. How about if we start

all over again from square one. I'd really like us to be friends."

Meredith felt her resolve melting at his gentle, coaxing tone. Hesitating briefly, she finally nodded. "I'd like that too, Jeff. I don't care for all this tension between us."

"Good! Then it's settled. Dinner tonight?"

Meredith paused, remembering their last date. Perhaps it would not be such a good idea. But if she said no, he'd take it as an insult and things would get worse.

"Well?"

"All right. Make it seven-thirty?"

"Seven-thirty it is."

The rest of the day passed slowly. Jeff was constantly in her thoughts. To her own amazement, she found herself wondering what it would be like to make love with him. She could see herself in his arms, feeling the possessiveness of his kisses...

"Ma'am, what should we do with it?"

Startled back into reality, Meredith saw a young man standing in front of her, holding her telephone link to the computer in Carmel. The small suitcase was heavy, as she well knew.

"I'm sorry! I never even heard you!"

"Yes, ma'am, but where shall I set this?"

Quickly clearing some space on her desk, she pointed. The sailor, placing it down, exhaled loudly. "Thank you, ma'am. Is there anything else you'll need?"

She looked at his flushed face and, feeling contrite, shook her head. "Look, I am sorry. How about if I buy you a cup of coffee?"

"That won't be necessary," he said with a tiny smile.

"All right. In that case, thank you for bringing it."

When quitting time neared, Meredith began to

gather her things. Backing away from her desk, she took one last glance around the room. Not looking behind her, she slammed into Mike who was just entering her office.

Mike grinned as she stumbled and grabbed on to the edge of her desk.

"Where did you come from?" she demanded.

"Just walked in. Didn't know my mere entrance would knock you for a loop. Well, that should confirm for you that I'm not exactly graceful.... I was wondering if you'd have dinner with me tonight."

Meredith smiled, pleased by the attention and flattered he had asked. He seemed so terribly shy, yet she knew he would deny the fact if confronted with it. Somehow it didn't fit the image he tried so hard to project.

"I'm sorry, but I've already made plans for tonight. Can I take a rain check?"

"Sure. How about tomorrow?"

"I'd like that."

They agreed on a time, and Meredith left the office in an especially good mood. She was glad Mike had asked her out. Perhaps this would distract her from her crazy preoccupation with Jeff. Mike was handsome and yet perfectly harmless, to her at least. Meredith grinned, thinking of what Mike's reaction would be if he could read her thoughts.

After a bath and a short nap, Meredith felt refreshed. This was her first free weekend in San Diego; she intended to relax and have fun. Deciding to keep the evening casual, in hopes it would make her more at ease with Jeff, she selected a light blue pantsuit and a white cotton turtleneck sweater. She applied makeup, working long on her eyes, then rose and pivoted slowly in front of the mirror. She gave her image the A-OK sign. She'd achieved just the effect she'd wanted. After carefully setting her hair with steam curlers, she combed the tight curls out. Her hair shone under the lights and fell softly around her shoulders.

A knock at her door signaled Jeff's arrival. Early this time, she thought with a smile. Opening the door, she stepped aside and asked him into the room. "Let me get a few things together and I'll be ready to go."

"Sure. There's no rush." Jeff glanced around. The room was spacious and equipped with all the little luxuries she could possibly want. The thick, plush pile carpeting, covering every inch of floor space, sank beneath his feet. "Hey, you must be pretty important to merit a place like this. You should see the ones they give me when I travel."

"Don't you stay in officers' quarters?"

"They're not always vacant, and when they're not available you take what you can get. It can be pretty grim."

"Aw, poor baby, roughing it in one of America's modern travel inns!"

"Well, I certainly don't get rooms like this one."

"And here I thought you were a real VIP. I've got to meet some of the big honchos and stop dating the small stuff."

"Ah, but wait and see what a good time this peon can show a lady."

Meredith chuckled softly. She had been pleased to see him looking more casual than last time. It seemed that his choice of clothing, too, had been made to help put them on more relaxed terms. His tan slacks and cream shirt, which he had left partially opened, were casual, though beautifully tailored. His brown leather jacket gave him an air of decided elegance, though. She was glad he had not chosen to wear neck chains or a medallion, which were so popular with men nowadays. Somehow she had never grown accustomed to them. They never seemed right.

"Okay. I'm ready when you are."

"Then let's go," he said.

Jeff led the way to his car, then paused after starting the engine. "What do you feel like eating?"

"You know what I'd really like? A pizza."

"You're on."

Jeff drove to a nearby pizza parlor, and this time, in the casual setting, their conversation flowed easily. How handsome he was! Her eyes slid down to the open-necked shirt. His powerful shoulders and muscular build were accentuated by his choice of clothing. Yet what she felt was more than a physical attraction. Something about him made her feel more feminine and more a woman. Hearing the secretaries at the base discuss him one morning during their coffee break, she wasn't surprised to learn she was not the only one who found him wildly attractive.

Jeff, almost as if reading her thoughts, reached out and covered her hand with his. The firmness of his grip surprised her but, despite his strength, there was a gentle quality in his touch. A tremor of pleasure rippled through her. This time she caressed his hand, enjoying the electricity physical contact with him produced. Abruptly, though, she pulled back.

Waiting for him to finish his beer while she drank her Coke, she tried to think of the right words to say. "Jeff, I..." Shaking her head, she looked down at her lap.

"Go on."

"Never mind."

"You were going to say something. Tell me."

"All right, Jeff. I'm not going to try and play games with you. You'd see right through them. If what you want is a one-night stand or...or a brief affair, I'm not what you're looking for. I've been hurt before and I never want to go through anything like that again. All I can offer you is friendship, but I can be a very good friend."

"That's all I want," Jeff answered.

"Honest? I don't want you to think I'm teasing you or being coy. I'm sure you can sense I'm attracted to you, but I have no intention of letting anything come of it. It's bad for business. I've got a job to do and I can't let personal feelings interfere with it. Do you understand?"

"Meredith, you're too uptight. Relax. I haven't asked anything of you, and I won't. Let's just enjoy each other's company and let things take their course."

"All right."

When Jeff smiled at her, Meredith saw his eyes soften. Perhaps they could be friends after all.

"Let me show you some more of San Diego. Have you ever seen the lighthouse?"

"No."

Once inside the small sports car, Meredith felt less pressured and began to talk freely. "I absolutely love your car."

"Thank you."

"Will you let me drive it sometime?"

Laughing, Jeff pulled off to the side of the road. "How about right now?"

"Really? Terrific!" Meredith's face lit up.

Jeff grinned as he helped her behind the wheel.

Meredith felt the purr of the engine as she shifted into low gear. Driving on the narrow road, she felt the car respond to the slightest pressure of the gas pedal. The car cornered beautifully on the winding coastal road. After driving for about thirty minutes, she pulled over. "Thanks, Jeff. I really enjoyed that."

"You can drive longer if you'd like."

"No, that's okay. I appreciate you letting me, but I know it made you nervous. I couldn't help but notice how your foot automatically kept reaching for the brake."

Laughing, Jeff switched places with her and eased

behind the wheel. Soon Meredith could see the tall white building by the water's edge.

"Is that it?" she asked.

"Yes. Wait until you see the view from the tower!"

Jeff led the way up the circular stairway. Looking all around her, Meredith marveled at the view. "Jeff, this is fabulous! Thanks so much for bringing me here."

He smiled, then looped his arm around her waist and brought her a little closer to him. Meredith stiffened almost immediately. Feeling her tenseness, he released her and walked around the circular guardrail. Small boats sailed around the bay as the moon illuminated the entire area.

In silence they returned to the car. Crossing a deeply shadowed area, Meredith lost her footing and started to fall backward. Jeff, instantly alert, caught her close and saved her from a tumble.

Meredith, suddenly pressed against him, fought a momentary panic. Mumbling something incoherent, she moved away. "Thanks. It would have ruined my image if I had fallen flat on my backside."

"Again, you mean, don't you?" he said teasingly.

"That time was on my face," she retorted lightly. "Now I'll have to come to your rescue sometime. Fair's fair, you know."

"Far be it from me to keep you from paying me back in kind."

"I can see you're a firm supporter of women's lib."

"Let me have your hand. It's dark and easy to trip." He chuckled. "If you prefer, I can let you take my hand and then we can say you were keeping *me* from breaking a leg."

"I'll make a deal with you. I'll hold your hand and you lead. That way if there's a hole or something to trip us up, you'll go first."

"That's my girl!"

Meredith found it hard to keep a straight face when he offered her his hand, much like a medieval lady waiting for a courtly kiss.

"Are you sure you can handle all this physical contact?" she asked.

"Watch it, or I'll push you into a hole myself."

After returning to the car, Jeff suggested a drive along the coastline. With the radio turned to soft music, Meredith felt completely at ease.

"You know, this is going to be a new experience for me," he said.

"What?"

"I've never had a woman as a friend before."

"You're kidding."

"No, seriously. Then again, in my kind of work we move around a lot and there's never any time to really make friends."

"You have friends on base. . . ."

"Sure, but I mean regular friends. Someone like you, for instance."

"Think you can deal with it?"

"There are temptations, you know."

"Naw. Just think of me as one of the guys."

Jeff laughed, then glanced at her face, then slowly lowered his eyes, allowing them to linger on her breasts briefly. "Hard to resist such a terrific looking fellow."

"Oh, it's men that attract you! Heavens, why didn't you say so? I'm sure we can find you a more suitable companion on the base. That way you won't have to fantasize when you're with me."

"Keep it up, and I'll really give you a sample of my fantasies."

"Sounds ominous."

"Care to try?"

"Well, let's see. I said you should try to treat me like one of the guys. Now you want to show me what you fantasize about.... I'm not sure if my delicate nature is ready for all of this, sir."

"Meri, there's an awful cold ocean out there. You may find yourself going for an unexpected swim."

"Now you're a bully!"

"You're offending my macho image!"

"Well, I promise I'll keep our conversation a secret."

"Meri, I'm warning you...."

Suddenly Jeff turned off to the side of the road, parking the car well off the pavement.

Meredith giggled, then lowered her head in mock sorrow. "I have deeply wronged you, oh handsome Commander. You are most certainly virile and ever a model of all masculinity."

"That's it!" Jeff pushed the car door on his side open. Reacting instantly, Meredith was off running on the sand. Her laughter sailed clearly over the crisp night air. She gained a few yards then, unexpectedly, Jeff turned and ran toward his car.

Confused, Meredith stopped and watched. Jeff jumped into his car, started the engine, and began to pull away. Meredith stared in wide-eyed horror. He couldn't really plan to leave her here!

Running, she sped toward his car only to find it pulling away. Her mouth opened slightly, as if to speak. Suddenly Jeff put the car into reverse and quickly backed up next to her.

"Scared you, huh?"

Meredith just nodded, a bit shaken by his joke. Seeing the look in her eyes, Jeff left the car and placed his arms around her. "Hey, silly, I wasn't really going to leave you here!"

Meredith swallowed and tried to keep her voice level. "Of course. I knew that all the time."

"Liar!" Jeff teased.

"That's one of my most charming qualities, didn't you know?"

"How about going for a walk?"

"Sure."

The deserted beach was edged with large rocks that jutted out into the sea, but the sand was cool and tempting. She kicked off her shoes. The crusty, damp sand felt good under her bare feet. As a breeze stirred, her hair whipped into her eyes. Jeff, smiling, gently pushed it from her face, hooking the long strands behind her ears.

"There. Now you can see. You were beginning to look like a sheep dog."

"Wonderful. I always wanted to be called a dog."

"New experience?"

"Of course. I'm a model of feminine beauty and charm."

"Oh? I hadn't noticed."

She shrugged. "Well, of course not. I mean, if your preferences lie elsewhere...."

Spinning her around, Jeff pulled her toward him. His laughing mouth came down on hers. Her pulse leaped wildly as he pressed her against him. Feeling her respond, Jeff kissed her hungrily and passionately, no longer with any restraint. Meredith allowed a soft moan to escape her as a maze of conflicting emotions exploded inside her.

Breathlessly she drew back and stared at him in dismay. "No more. Leave me alone!"

"Meredith, what's wrong with you? The way you respond to me and I respond to you is nothing short of total. Why fight it?"

"Jeff, listen to me and please try to understand. I want us to be *friends*. We work very closely together. I can't get so emotionally involved with you; I won't be able to do my job properly. Please, don't make it harder for me than it is already."

Jeff began walking toward the car. "Meri, are you sure it's only because of the reasons you just stated, or is there something you're not saying?"

"I don't understand. . . ."

"Meredith, forgive me if I seem to be prying, but, honey, it looks to me like you're just man shy. What did that other guy do to you?"

"How did you . . ." Meredith stammered. She took a deep breath and forced herself to relax. "I don't want to talk about it. I'm mixed up right now and I really couldn't offer anything to a relationship anyway."

"Why don't you let me be the judge of that?"

"No, Jeff. This isn't negotiable. I'm afraid it's my way or nothing."

"All right. I sure wish I could make you trust me a bit more. I'm not Attila the Hun, you know."

Meredith snapped her fingers in mock realization. "That's who you remind me of. Of course!"

"I suppose I stepped right into that," Jeff replied resignedly. Seeing her shiver, he removed his jacket and placed it over her shoulders.

"You don't have to do that, Jeff. Now you'll be cold."

"Naw. Us Huns never get cold."

"Well, then it's all right. Your skin would look better next to a soft shade of blue, anyway."

They drove back to the hotel in silence, listening to the music from the radio. Meredith's thoughts were in a jumble. What was it about him that appealed to her so? She wanted him, yet she knew she could never allow herself that luxury—not just out of moral principle but also because of the *depth* of Jeff's appeal. Mark had taken too much from her and left too little behind. If it happened again, she would not have the strength to deal with it. The rejection, the hurt. . . . She still remembered the long sleepless nights, how her work had suffered from her lack of ability to concentrate. And that terrified her. Time had made the hurt from Mark's betrayal less painful, but the sick feeling in the pit of her stomach still remained.

Meredith had promised herself no other man would ever capture her heart, but now Jeff was in her life. With that strength and amusement in his eyes, the physical magnetism made every nerve in her body come alive.

"Okay, beautiful lady, we're back." Jeff parked the car close to the entrance, then escorted her inside.

As they waited for the elevator, Meredith returned his jacket. "Thanks. It was a very nice gesture."

"My pleasure."

"And thanks again for everything. Really."

"How about tomorrow night at seven-thirty?"

"You sure you want to?"

"I wouldn't ask if I didn't."

"Okay." Meredith paused, then slapped her forehead lightly. "Wait, I forgot. I can't. I've made plans."

"Who's taking you out tomorrow?" Jeff asked, instantly alert.

"Mike."

"Works fast, doesn't he?"

"Look who's talking. You did, after all, ask me out for tonight...."

"That's different."

"Uh huh. Come on, Jeff, I thought we had agreed to keep things on a friendly basis. I can see whoever I want and so can you! Let's not complicate things."

"Whatever you say." With a glance as cold as ice, Jeff turned and walked away. Never looking behind him, he strode to the parking lot and out of sight.

The next morning, with no alarm to wake her, Meredith slept. Neither the sound of traffic nor the morning breakfast carts being pushed up and down the halls evoked a response from her. As the sun began its ascent into the morning sky, it filtered through an opening in the curtains. The golden light played upon her pillow, touching her face and slowly nudging her awake. Smiling, she stretched lazily. It was good to be able to relax and not have to rush to work. Too bad she hadn't been born wealthy. She would have been perfectly suited to a life of leisure. Placing her hands behind her head, she kicked the covers from her body and then lay still. Well, she would have to get up sooner or later, and there was much she wanted to do. Slowly getting out of bed, she walked to the closet and stood there, trying to decide what to wear. The telephone jangled. Placing her hand on the receiver, she hesitated. Surely it wouldn't be Jeff. She shook her head as if to clear the confusion in her thoughts. Half of her wished it might be he, the other half fervently hoped it was not. Heaving a sigh, she picked it up.

"Meredith?"

"Yes."

"This is Mike. Do you like horses?"

"I love horses, why?"

"I have a terrific idea, that is if you're free this morning. A friend of mine owns a couple of thoroughbreds. The stable boy who normally exercises them by the beach didn't come in and they still need to be taken out. How about it?"

Meredith's eyes lit up. "Mike, that's an absolutely marvelous idea. I would love it!"

"Pick you up in an hour?"

"Yes!"

She showered and made up in record time, then stepped into a pair of jeans and a long-sleeved blouse. Although the neck plunged a bit more than she would've preferred, it was perfect for a day outdoors—cool and extremely comfortable. Feeling excited at the prospect of riding, Meredith went downstairs.

After stopping at the coffee shop long enough to

pick up a doughnut and a cup of coffee, she walked to the lobby. Within minutes, Mike appeared.

"Good morning! Don't tell me you haven't even had breakfast yet! It's ten-thirty!"

"Just finished," she said laughing, as she licked the icing from her fingers. "Thanks for asking me, Mike. I love horseback riding. How did you know?"

"Oh, I thought you looked the type."

"Well, whatever that means, I'm glad you thought of me."

Driving along, Meredith thought about the difference between Mike and Jeff. With Mike she was completely at ease. She did not feel pressured or threatened in any way. The morning held great promise. She eagerly anticipated doing the one thing she loved most in the world. Even flying took a second to riding.

Soon they arrived at the stable. It seemed an eternity before Mike found a space and parked the car. Anticipation and excitement showed clearly on Meredith's face. Leading the way inside the stables, Mike stopped at the stall of a beautiful chestnut stallion. The animal, eager for his long-overdue exercise, pranced around, then whinnied.

Laughing, Meredith stroked his beautiful, muscular neck. Responding to her attention, the animal lowered its head and buried it against Meredith's chest.

"Well, that's that. He likes you. I'll take the other one."

"Wait, we're not actually riding them, right? We'll ride another pair and lead these two along, isn't that the normal procedure?"

"It is, but I asked my friend, and he thought this once it wouldn't do any harm. Just be careful. They're pretty frisky."

"No problem. I've ridden horses practically since I could walk."

After saddling the huge animals, they walked them toward the beach, then mounted and took off in a trot. Meredith couldn't keep a smile off her face. The sound of the sea, the warmth of the sun, and the energy of the thoroughbred beneath her made her spirits soar. Soon, not to tire the animals, they slowed to a walk. Mike pulled his horse next to hers. Continuing down the beach at a comfortable pace, Meredith smiled in thanks to the man beside her.

"I'm glad this was such a success with you."

"Oh, Mike! I haven't had this much fun in ages!"

They rode in silence. Then, without any warning, Mike pulled the reins on his horse and came to an abrupt stop. "Meredith, there's something I have to ask you."

"Anything."

"Is there something between you and Jeff? I heard talk around the hangar and I wondered..."

"There's nothing between Jeff and me. But I sure would be interested to know what you heard."

"It's nothing. You know how people talk."

"Mike, please. I really need to know. I promise no one will learn you told me."

"The men made a bet on how long it'll take Jeff to make you one of his conquests."

"That's disgusting."

"You wanted to know."

"I work with the man day in and day out, and we've gone out a couple of times, that's all."

Mike became oddly quiet. In a strange tone of voice, he added, "I'm glad, for your sake."

"What's that supposed to mean?"

"Surely you're aware that he's a master of the 'sweep them off their feet, sweep them out the door' number."

"No, I didn't know that."

"Believe me, Meredith, don't take anything he tells

you at face value. He's good with women, almost too smooth, but I have to admit he's a number-one success at getting what he wants from them."

Meredith's eyebrows furrowed. Thank God she hadn't totally lowered her guard! Now it made sense. The insistence, the woman at the restaurant, and the pressure he put on her. Another couple of weeks, if he had gotten what he had been after, he would have left her and she would have had to pick up the pieces. From now on there would be no more dates, no more anything, unless it was strictly business. Besides, she was having a much nicer time with Mike. Yet, undeniably, the thought of not seeing Jeff again made her very sad.

"You're miles away."

"Sorry, Mike. I didn't mean to be."

Smiling mischievously, she spurred her horse forward at a gallop, leaving him to catch up. Instantly aware of the game, Mike gave chase. The animals eagerly leaped forward, straining against the metal bits in their mouths. Meredith, sensing her stallion's fiery spirit, loosened her hold on the reins, allowing the horse to gallop at full speed. The animals snorted as the excitement of the race infected them. The air whipped against Meredith's hair as the sand flew beneath the horses' hoofs. Although both stallions appeared equally matched, Mike's superior knowledge of his own mount allowed him to catch up. Slowing their pace, they walked the horses for another mile along the water's edge before returning them to the stable.

"Mike, it was a perfect morning!"

"It was fun, wasn't it?"

Meredith allowed Mike to help her off the horse, although she needed no assistance. After putting the saddles away they picked up a couple of brushes and began to smooth the stallions' wet coats. Slipping a blanket over each animal's back, they secured them into place and led their mounts in a circle to cool them down. After a few minutes they brought the horses back into their stalls.

"You hungry?" Mike inquired.

"Absolutely!"

"I have a great idea. Let's go to Old Town."

"What's that?"

"You've never seen it? Then you're in for a treat. That is, if you don't mind doing some walking."

"Not at all."

Grinning at each other with devilish twinkles in their eyes, they raced back to the car. Soon they were underway. Meredith was thankful she had made such a good friend. She liked Mike's casual air now and was glad he was no longer shy around her.

As the car turned into a spacious parking area, Meredith could see a row of picturesque shops and adobe buildings ahead. A tribute to California's first city, Old Town was six and a half blocks of Old Mexico. The little shops offered almost everything imaginable for sale. Stopping at a colorful Mexican restaurant, they sat in one of the umbrella-topped tables.

Meredith glanced at the menu and grimaced. "Mike, I don't know what to order. I'm not too familiar with this type of food. Will you order for me?"

"Sure."

When the waiter arrived, Mike placed their order. Soon a tray full of *sopapillas* was brought. The fried bread, typical of Mexican delicacies, was excellent. Meredith, copying Mike's lead, liberally laced the top of the biscuit with honey. The bread, light and airy, almost melted in her mouth.

Enjoying a leisurely meal, and encouraged by the setting, Mike talked freely, telling Meredith about himself. No trace of the self-consciousness he had displayed earlier remained.

"How long have you been a pilot?" Meredith asked.

"Ever since I joined up. That's been about six years now. I knew I wanted to fly, so I enlisted as a naval aviator. When I was offered the opportunity to test some of the aircraft the Navy would be using, I jumped at the chance."

"Doesn't it make it hard on you, the way they keep moving you around from one place to another?"

"Sometimes. It is hard to form any lasting relationships that way. I never seem to be in one place long enough."

"Is that what you want? A lasting relationship?"

"I think I'm ready for it now. I'd like to have a home and family."

"You're a very handsome man and a very eligible bachelor. I'm sure you wouldn't have any lack of applicants for the position."

"Are you applying?"

"Me?" Meredith, startled, began to laugh. "I should scare the dickens out of you and say yes."

"Oh, I don't think I'd be exactly terror stricken."

"You'd probably go pale and head for the hills."

"Try me," he responded with a wide grin.

"No, I don't think I will. Not yet, anyway."

"Now who's afraid?"

Meredith hit him playfully over the head with the dessert menu. "Stinker!"

"What about you? Will you always be strictly a career woman?"

"I really don't know. I do love my job, though. There's always something interesting happening."

"You don't think about getting married and having a family?"

"Yes, sometimes. I just keep changing my mind.

Sometimes I think it would be lovely, then other times I think that to give up the freedom to do what I want, whenever I want, I'd have to be crazy."

Mike smiled. "I know exactly what you mean."

Meredith stared down at the empty plate for a few minutes, then spoke softly, almost in a whisper. "I also never want to allow anyone to get so close to me that . . ." Meredith looked up, aware she had said too much. "I'm sorry. I didn't mean to get into that."

"Tell me what happened." His eyes softened and he reached over the table, covering her hand with his. "Tell me."

Meredith hesitated. Sensing, more than hearing, the understanding and friendship he offered, she continued. "Mark and I were quite an item for almost a year. He had asked me to marry him and I had accepted. Then, as the time neared, he asked whether I would postpone the date. He said he needed more time. I agreed. He began to drift away from me. I could sense it but I couldn't do anything about it. Finally, one day he told me he had accepted a job in Canada. I thought he meant for both of us to go, but he had made it quite clear that he no longer felt the same and that he wanted out. Something about having no strings attached to him. I didn't think I'd make it through that, but somehow I did—and here I am. I'll admit there wasn't much left after he went away, but I finally got myself together. I'll never allow that to happen to me again."

"Meredith, you can't let that stop you from trying again with another man. You'll only end up hurting yourself."

"I can't help it. I'm not sure I could stand another rejection like that. It was pure hell afterward. For every pleasant moment I shared with him there were many hours of pain."

"Yes, I know."

Meredith, alerted by the changed tone in his voice, looked up. Mike now glanced away at the distance, as if a million miles away.

"It may not change things, but I'll listen," she said, giving his hand a gentle squeeze.

Mike focused his attention once more on her. "It wasn't too long ago. I was engaged. She was everything a man could want—beautiful, loving, and caring. Everything was going fine, when I received orders to go on sea duty. She knew my job would require that from time to time, so she wasn't overly upset. We had planned on having the wedding as soon as I returned. In six months she was to become my wife. I had been gone four and a half months when I received a letter from her. It was nice and simple. She had found someone else, so good-bye. It was like having someone kick you in the stomach. The worst part of it was I couldn't talk it over with anyone."

"You mean it was too painful?"

"Well, that too, but the main reason was I could have been grounded. If what had happened had become public knowledge, some idiot in the medical department could have grounded me, saying my mental condition made me a potential hazard. I didn't want to lose her and my wings too."

"I can understand that."

"Then, after I had been back for about a month, she came over to my apartment. The guy had apparently become bored of the game and dumped her. She wanted me to take her back."

"What did you do?"

"I told her she had made her decision and that I wanted nothing more to do with her."

"She really put your through the wringer, didn't she?" Meredith's eyes mirrored her compassion. She knew exactly how he had felt and how hard it was to leave the past behind.

"Look, it's a beautiful day! How did we ever get on this subject anyway?" he said.

"Who knows!"

"Are you finished?" he asked, still holding on to her hand.

"Yes. Shall we go?"

Mike walked around the table and helped Meredith up. Throwing his arm about her shoulders, they continued to walk around the plaza, glancing inside store windows.

"Shall I take you back to the hotel, then pick you up for dinner, or would you like to go for a long drive with me?"

"A drive sounds terrific," Meredith said.

"It's still early. How would you like to go up into the mountains? I know a beautiful spot in the San Gabriels."

"Okay. Sounds good to me."

Mike drove rather slowly, knowing the day was theirs to spend as they wished. Mesmerized by the beat of rock sounds from the radio, Meredith allowed her mind to drift aimlessly as she enjoyed the ever-changing scene through her window. How marvelous to be with Mike! None of the jumble of emotions she felt around Jeff was present when she was with him. But, of course, the violent swirl of emotions Jeff aroused in her and the magnetic attraction between them was something she was unlikely to experience with anyone else. Even Mark had not stirred her that way. There was something unique there. Something special, yet extremely dangerous to her. She was much safer and much better off in Mike's company.

Mike reached over and ruffled her hair playfully. She smiled. With Mike it was like having a big brother to talk things over with and pass the time of day.

As the sun began to sink over the horizon, she tried to suppress a yawn.

"Tired?"

"Yes. I think I've had it for today. But you know what? I haven't had this much fun since I was a kid."

"Me too."

Meredith struggled to keep awake during the trip back to San Diego. Finally admitting to herself she would make an abominable dinner companion, she decided to sound him out. "I'm having trouble keeping awake."

"I've noticed that. May I make a suggestion?"

"Shoot."

"How about I take you back to the hotel. I'm pretty beat myself. We'll skip dinner and make it tomorrow night."

"You've read my mind again. Thanks. I think it's a marvelous idea."

When they arrived at Meredith's hotel, Mike escorted her in. He waited until she opened her door, then gave her a gentle kiss. It was pleasant, but kindled no flames.

"See you tomorrow night."

"What time?"

"Seven?"

"Fine." Meredith gratefully saw him leave. She hated the scenes where she felt compelled to ask the man inside. She didn't really like to do that, yet sometimes it was almost embarrassing not to. Mike, too considerate to put her in an awkward situation, had quietly left. Why couldn't all men be like that?

Intending to take a short nap, bathe, and go to sleep, Meredith disconnected the telephone, switched off the lights, and laid atop the bed, fully clothed.

Before she knew it, it was morning.

# - 4 -

THE BREEZE RUSTLED through the trees outside Meredith's window as she rubbed her eyes. Slowly peering out through sleepy lashes, she heard the sound of muffled laughter echoing from the corridor. With a sigh, she turned toward the night stand, searching for the clock. It couldn't be! Meredith shut her eyes hard, then opened them once again. It was ten o'clock! Reconnecting the telephone, she ordered coffee and rolls from room service, then sat on the edge of the bed and tried to force herself awake. The telephone suddenly interrupted the stillness of the darkened room. Muttering under her breath, she picked up the receiver.

"Hello," she mumbled.

"Meredith, where have you been? I've been trying to call you since yesterday morning!"

"Jeff?"

"Of course, Jeff! Who were you expecting?"

"Jeff, have a heart, will you? I just woke up."

"Out carousing all night?"

"Oh shut up." Meredith, not waiting for a reply, put the receiver back on its cradle.

Hearing a knock, Meredith smoothed her wrinkled shirt, then opened the door. Smiling, she stood back while a young waiter brought in a cart containing hot coffee and rolls. The enticing aroma made her hungry. The waiter picked up one of the chairs and placed it by the table.

"Thanks," she said. Handing him a tip, she waited until he left the room. Somehow he had managed to make her feel nervous. Sitting down, she began to eat. The coffee had been freshly brewed and tasted delicious. Its rich aromatic smell filled the room, adding a distinct and pleasant touch to her morning. She was delighted with herself to have thought of ordering room service. Nibbling on a roll, she felt guilty about having hung up on Jeff. But it was too late to do anything about it now. Calmly sipping the steaming coffee, she allowed her thoughts to drift. Her date with Mike had been lovely. He was such a sweet man. She was glad he had warned her about Jeff. Now she'd be extra careful. She would never fall prey to any of his lies.

Pushing her chair back, she stood and glanced around the room. The first order of business of the day was a bath, then she'd look over some paperwork before taking the rest of the day off.

Carrying the coffee cup into the bathroom, she turned on the tap and watched the warm water fill the tub. As soon as it reached the level she desired, she slipped out of her clothes and stepped in. Placing the cup on the rim of the bathtub, she relaxed, enjoying the luxury of her leisurely pace. It was then she heard a loud banging on her door. Meredith rolled her eyes impatiently, then paused, trying to decide what to do. Opting to ignore it, she laid back and relaxed. Her eyes had closed momentarily as she tried to shut everything out, when a voice boomed from the hallway.

"Meredith, open the door. I know you're in there. I saw your car!"

Jeff! What in the world did he think he was doing? Had he completely lost his mind? Meredith quickly stepped out of the tub and wrapped a towel around herself. Walking into the room, she edged up to the door. "Jeff, be quiet! I was in the bathtub, you idiot! Go away and let me finish my bath."

"I want to talk to you now."

"Jeff, for God's sake, lower your voice! I'm not dressed. Go away for a while, then come back."

"I'll yell at the top of my lungs if you don't let me talk to you."

"Jeff, please!"

"I want to talk to you, Meredith. Open this door!"

"All right! Look, I'll unlock it, but wait half a minute before you come in. That will give me time to find some clothes." Meredith unlocked the door, but before she had taken more than a few steps, Jeff burst inside. Angrily, Meredith spun around. "What do you think you're doing?"

"First of all, don't hang up on me—ever! It could have been important. I don't appreciate temper tantrums!"

"You've got some sense of humor. You pull a stunt like this, then come read me the riot act?"

Jeff smiled. "My, my! We do sleep late after an all-nighter."

"All-nighter? Jeff, I'm warning you, either get out or I'll scream the place down."

"I thought you wanted to be friends."

"I've reconsidered. Get out."

"You look lovely, but don't you think you better get dressed before you tempt me too much?"

"If you're trying to make me angry, you're succeeding."

"All I want is to take you to lunch. How about it?"

"Out! Right this minute! Out!"

"You won't give me the time of day, but you spent most of the night, or is it all night, with Mike?"

"That's none of your business, mister," Meredith said in an ominously quiet voice.

"Don't I even rate a lunch date?"

"Leave."

"Damn it, Meri, this is turning out all wrong. All I wanted to do is to spend some time with you. Look, let me make it up to you." Jeff pulled her toward him. Out of balance, Meredith's hands instinctively flew out in front of her. She felt the tucked-in corner that held the towel around her slip as she attempted to push away from him. Suddenly the towel came loose, falling freely around her feet. Jeff's eyes slid downward.

"Meredith," he murmured, loosening his hold. "You're absolutely breathtaking!"

"You toad! You insufferable bully!" she yelled, quickly recovering her towel. "Get out of this room, right now!"

"All right, damn it! If it's Mike you prefer, then you can have him, but let me give you a friendly warning. Mike knows women, Meredith. You're no match for him."

"I don't prefer Mike!" Meredith shook her head angrily. "What am I doing? I don't owe you any explanation! You burst in here like King Kong, you don't give me a chance to throw a robe on, and then you have the gall to tell me to worry about him? You've got some nerve!"

Jeff smiled as if her revelation that she didn't prefer Mike made him number one in the running. "Well, now we're even. You walked in on me, remember? And we were just strangers then!"

In a fit of fury, Meredith backed up two paces, then picked up a huge vase on her dresser. "You . . . you rat!" Holding on to the towel with one hand, she swung the vase, ready to throw it at him.

Jeff, seeing she had every intention of carrying out her threat, beat a nasty retreat, slamming the door shut to the unmistakable crash of glass shattering against it.

Meredith threw the towel down onto the floor with a fury, then walked back to the tub. Lowering herself into the lukewarm water, with the intention of continuing where she had left off, she leaned back and closed her eyes. Slowly, anger gave way to embarrassment. How humiliating! She had been left completely bare to his gaze, and he hadn't missed an inch! Well, he did have incredibly good taste, she thought with a grin. After all, he had said she was breathtaking!

Thinking of the incident, Meredith felt a twinge of excitement pulse through her. She could still feel his eyes taking in every curve on her body. God, what was it about him that stirred her so? Even her own body fought against her, as desire gave way to longing. No, this wouldn't do. He had acted like a total boor and she would neither forgive nor forget. She stepped out of the tub and dried herself. This morning's serenity was gone; it was no use trying to recapture it. Wrapping her robe around her, she tiptoed around, careful not to cut her feet as she picked up the shattered glass and threw the pieces into the trash.

Meredith finished dressing and had just begun combing her hair when a knock sounded on her door. Oh, no! If that was him, she'd kill him! Determined to stand her ground, she strode to the door and threw it open.

"Well, what now?" Instantly contrite, she looked into the face of a young boy. "Oh! I'm so sorry! I thought you were someone else!"

Picking up a huge bouquet of flowers he had set by his feet, he handed them to her. "Ma'am, these are for you."

Meredith's eyes grew wide with amazement as she looked at the immense arrangement of red roses and baby's breath. "They're gorgeous! But are you sure they're for me?"

"Meredith Buchanan?"

"That's me! Wait, let me get something for you."

"No, ma'am. The gentleman already took care of that."

"What gentleman?" Meredith asked, looking down the empty corridor.

"The one who ordered those."

Meredith accepted the flowers and turned to place them on the table. Eager to ask more questions, she glanced toward the hall, but the boy was gone. Closing the door, she walked back to the table. The roses were exquisite. A small white envelope was balanced on top of the bouquet. Tearing it open, she pulled the card out.

To my beautiful lady friend. Will my efforts merit at least one tiny smile?
Jeff

Meredith smiled, despite herself. The roses were lovely. Well, she would let him stew awhile before forgiving him. After all, he had acted terribly. Placing the roses in the remaining vase, she touched the petals lightly. Jeff could be so infuriating yet so sensitive when he wanted to be. He was quite a package.

After she opened the curtains to let the sunshine in, Meredith sat back and studied the new data on the

Scorpio. There would be another test flight in a few days and she wanted to be prepared. An hour or so into her work, she heard another knock on her door. Thinking it was Jeff, she stopped in front of the mirror to check her appearance, then opened the door.

The same young boy stood in front of her, holding another massive spray, only this time the roses were yellow. "I think you made a mistake. Remember, you brought some flowers to me not too long ago," Meredith said.

"No, ma'am. There's no mistake. These are for you."

"Well, at least let me get something for you."

"No, ma'am. The gentleman already took care of that."

Laughing, Meredith received the second bouquet and took them inside her room. The flowers were exquisite. Placing them on the night stand, she dialed room service and asked that a vase be sent up. Glancing at the new bouquet, she bit her lower lip absentmindedly. Perhaps she wouldn't let him stew terribly long.

Meredith returned to her paperwork after placing the yellow flowers in the new vase. Scowling, she tossed the papers back onto the desk. She needed to get out. Lunch at the boathouse restaurant everyone talked about seemed just the ticket. Part of another hotel, it was said to be charming. Freshening her makeup, she walked out to her car. She drove around, familiarizing herself with her surroundings. California's second-largest city had no shortage of interesting places. Yet her interest focused on the crescent-shaped bay around which San Diego was built. Boats were everywhere. The bay housed everything from pleasure craft to destroyers.

Driving along a palm-tree-lined freeway, she switched the radio on to a soft-music station and re-

laxed. She had the impression that the road was floating atop the bay. Seeing cars turn off to a crowded
marina, Meredith decided to follow their lead. The
sign said SHELTER ISLAND. Meredith parked her car
and walked to the water's edge. Tall masts seemed
to grow out of the water much like floating popsicle
sticks. Pleasure boats of all types and shapes were
huddled together in the crowded dock. Refusing the
invitations of three young men, she began to walk
back to her car. A slight breeze blew through her hair,
then she felt a faint spray of salt water moisten her
skin. It was a beautiful day!

As she returned to the freeway, she heard her stomach rumble in protest. Aware of her growing hunger,
she glanced at her watch. It was time to have lunch.

The boathouse restaurant was everything she had
expected. The small harbor around it was filled with
a myriad of pleasure craft. Men sporting luscious tans
milled about. Meredith chose a seat close to the large
paned windows. If one thing marked Californians, it
was their casual style.

Devouring a club sandwich, she amused herself
watching a small boy out on a sailboat, still docked
to the pier. He was obviously enjoying himself as he
pretended to fend off a hoard of imaginary pirates.
Meredith stifled a giggle as he lurched forward with
his make-believe sword, vanquishing his invisible
opponents.

Reluctantly, she paid her check and left. She
wanted to continue sightseeing, but she had work to
do. Heaving a sigh, she got into her car and drove
back to her hotel.

In front of her room, placed in a makeshift stack,
lay three long white boxes tied with bright ribbons.
Meredith's eyes gleamed with excitement. It was definitely her day. She picked up the boxes and carried
them inside her room. Slipping off the ribbon, she

opened the first box. As she parted the thin floral paper that covered it, she found one perfect red rose. The card, laid atop it, said simply, "Jeff."

Meredith moved to the second box and brought out a beautiful white rose. Not a blemish anywhere marred its purity. Again the card read, "Jeff."

Meredith moved toward the third box in eager anticipation. This time she found a red carnation. The card read, "Just a thought. What if my lady friend doesn't like roses?"

His attempts to placate her had pleased her. Picking up her address book, she found his number and then placed the call. No one answered. Meredith waited a few minutes, then placed her call again. Still no luck. With infinite care, she arranged the flowers in the vases with the others, then smiled.

Returning to her desk, she concentrated on the documents in front of her. An unexpected knock startled her. Glancing toward the door, she grinned playfully. She stood, walked to the door with deliberate slowness, then opened it. This time, holding a huge bottle of Harvey's Bristol Cream, was Jeff, looking much like a naughty little boy. Silently offering the bottle to her, he turned around and began walking away.

"Come back here, you dummy!"

Jeff turned back, a smile on his handsome face. "Your wish is my command."

"Well, you might as well come in," Meredith said.

"Only if I'm completely forgiven."

"You are forgiven."

Waiting for her to close the door, he stood inches away from her. "Do I get a kiss to make it all better?"

"Hey! I was the maligned party here, remember?"

"You know, you're absolutely right. *You* should get the kiss."

Jeff swept her against him. Meredith felt her resistance shatter under the gentle pressure of his lips.

Desire swept through her as she pressed against him, fitting her body against his. She could feel the hardness of his flesh as her hands caressed his rippling shoulders. Hesitantly, she pushed away from him.

Jeff looked down at her, eyes blazing with passion. "I won't do anything you don't want me to. Say 'stop' and I will! One more kiss now?"

Meredith trembled visibly. She wanted him but knew she could not, should not, have him.

Seeing her hesitate, Jeff smiled. "I must really mean something to you. Otherwise you wouldn't be afraid."

She took his dare. "Afraid," she echoed scornfully. "Don't flatter yourself." Stepping forward, Meredith placed her arms around his neck and slowly brought his face toward hers. Jeff, as if raw with desire, forced her mouth open, slipping his tongue between her lips. The probing insistence caused Meredith's knees to grow weak. Clutching him for support, she returned his fevered kisses. As his lips moved to her throat and neck, Meredith felt passion surge through her like a bolt of lightning. Matching his intensity, she returned his caresses and pressed closer against him. She felt the overpowering need to be possessed. She wanted the man who brought out these violent emotions to teach her all he knew about love.

Jeff pushed her back until she rested on the bed. He gently caressed her face while pressing urgent kisses on her mouth, chin, and throat. Whispering breathless endearments, he sensitized her skin with the magic of his touch. When his hand slid down to her breasts, she pressed forward eagerly. Moaning softly, she waited in anticipation as he opened her blouse with swift, sure movements and bared her breasts. Kissing each gently, he continued to fondle her. Meredith's body arched toward him in sweet agony. Feeling a fire grow hot inside her, Meredith pulled his head down toward her. His mouth opened, devouring the full ripeness of her nipple. The intimate stimulation caused her to quiver as a wild, incessant longing tore at the core of her being.

His hand dropped with infinite sureness to her hips, which he caressed with maddening strokes before easing to her zipper. He slid it down, stopping a few inches short of the bottom and exposing her navel. His fingers played teasingly over her flat stomach, making her writhe with tender agony and painful pleasure. Slowly, he stripped away the rest of her clothes until she lay fully exposed. He stood and looked down at her, devouring every inch of her flesh, and she reveled at the excitement in his eyes, the ragged raspiness of his breathing that the sight of her body inspired. Then he began to take off his clothes. He was neither hasty, as if in embarrassment, nor slow, as if showing himself off unduly. Rather, he was giving her the opportunity to savor him with her eyes as he'd savored her. And she watched with unblushing admiration for his body.

Meredith bit her lip as spasms of urgent desire coursed through her, then reached out and touched his powerful thigh muscles, her fingers thrilling to the feel of him.

"I need you so, Meredith." His voice was so husky it sounded almost like a growl. "If you say 'stop' now, I don't know if—"

"Come to me," she interrupted his tortured words. The purr in her voice and her outstretched arms seemed to break all his restraints. He moaned ecstatically and then lowered himself on her.

Once more his body moved in slow ritual awakening against her, his hands provoking delicious sensations in areas of her body she'd never before known to be erotically alive.

"You're driving me crazy," she murmured. "Crazy with wanting you."

"And you're making me wild," he muttered into her neck. Then, head rearing back with fierce grace, he stared down into her face with an expression of tender possession and gentle conquest.

"Please, now!" she cried. And they became one, soft sounds of animal pleasure escaping from their lips, each exciting the other to new heights . . . until they exploded together in a frenzied rapture.

Spent, they could say nothing and lay with arms and legs entwined, eyes tenderly probing one another. Finally, aglow and mellow, Meredith said, "I've never. known anything like that, Jeff."

"Neither have I, my sweet." He cradled her even closer. "You see? We belong together," he whispered into her hair. "Fighting it will only end up making us both miserable."

Blissfully content, she snuggled against him and drifted into light sleep.

Too soon she awakened in a panic. She felt as if she'd been drowning, and bolted to a sitting position, gasping for the breath of life.

"What is it, honey?" Jeff asked urgently, sitting up as quickly as she had.

She looked at him and suddenly saw a dangerous stranger, not an intimate lover.

"My God," he exclaimed. "You're looking at me like I'm some kind of predator. No, wait. More like I'm a lifeboat with a gusher of a leak in the middle of a rough sea." His lips curled in a slight smile.

She blinked. "I . . . I did feel like I was drowning." She shrugged away from the arm he put around her shoulders. She lowered her head into her hands. "Oh, Jeff. What have I done? Forgive me. This was all a terrible mistake!"

"No way, darlin'. It was absolutely right." His fingers found her chin and forced her face up and around so he could see her eyes. "What are you so worried about? What awful things do you think are going to happen now?"

Meredith turned away. "Nothing is going to happen now." Her voice held conviction.

"Maybe I've rushed you too much. You're going to need more time before you can deal with your feelings and emotions."

Jeff looked at her steadily, then with regret mirrored in his eyes, stood and dressed. "I'll give you as much time as you need, Meri. You're worth the wait," he said, then kissed her lightly on the forehead. He dressed, then walked out of her room, closing the door softly behind him.

Meredith, bewildered, looked around her for a few minutes, as if expecting the walls to answer her silent questions. As realization flooded through her, tears began to fall down her cheeks. If this was love, it was much too confusing. After releasing the pressure of pent-up emotions, she stood and walked to the bathroom sink. Washing the trail of tears from her face, she returned to the bedroom, slipped on a robe, and sat on the edge of the bed, deep in thought.

Why couldn't Jeff be more like Mike? Her times with him were pleasant and they always had fun. Jeff brought only confusion, yet she couldn't force him from her mind. The incredible magnetism between them seemed to permeate their lives and control their fate. She had to learn to keep a firm hold on things, to dissolve this power he had over her. What if she were completely and hopelessly in love with him and he tired of her...left her! What would she do then? No! She nearly shrieked the denial.

Meredith's face contorted in grim determination. "I'll fight you, Commander," she muttered, "you and this feeling that comes rushing to the surface every time you're near. I won't let you use me and discard me like that poor girl in the restaurant. I won't become one of your conquests!"

She jumped up, hurriedly showered, then threw on her clothes. Grabbing her purse, she rushed out of the confines of her room. She needed to get out in the open, to spend some time thinking, alone. This evening she would be with Mike, but the rest of the afternoon was hers. She would take a short drive and try to sort things out for herself. Longing for a change of pace from the hustle and bustle of the city, she decided to seek the serenity of the country. The scenery began to change slowly as she headed toward the peaceful farming and mining communities just outside the city. The freeway, winding its corkscrew course, afforded beautiful views of the agricultural valleys below. Wooden barns, dating back to the turn of the century, served as reminders of the past. The hills at the distance, rolling and stretching as far as the eye could see, were partially covered with a fine mist. Deep shades of blue and green covered the countryside in a delicate mantle of color.

It was with great reluctance that she headed back into town. She now regretted having promised to see Mike this evening. She had only just begun to enjoy her solitude. As Meredith drove past the sign heralding her entry into the city, she felt a twinge of sadness. She would have liked to continue driving for a week or so before returning. As she neared her hotel, she checked her watch. Time had passed quickly; she had barely fifteen minutes before Mike was supposed to meet her.

She parked quickly and ran through the lobby to the elevator. Making a short dash to her room, she changed her clothing and began the process of trying to arrange her hair. Tonight it seemed determined to do anything except what she wanted it to. Tying it back into a tight bun, she looked at her image in the mirror and frowned. It wouldn't do. Removing the pins, she allowed her hair to fall freely about her shoulders. She took a scarf from her suitcase, folded it lengthwise, then, using it as a headband, brushed her hair around it. As she stepped back to evaluate the outcome, a knock sounded at her door.

Meredith applied the final touch of powder and hurried out of her room. She stopped in the middle of the corridor. "Jeff! What are you doing here?"

Jeff greeted her with his self-assured smile. "You look gorgeous, as always. How about letting me take you to dinner?"

"I can't. I..." Meredith never had the chance to finish. Mike walked up and, with an air of confidence, placed his arm around her shoulders.

"Are you ready, pretty lady?"

Jeff's face turned a deep scarlet as he glared at his colleague. "You're asking for it, Mike," he growled softly.

"Jeff, surely you're not afraid of a little competition," Mike retorted in a casual tone.

Meredith, aware of the storm brewing and afraid that something would get started, stepped between the two of them. "Jeff, Mike had asked me out to dinner last night. I'm sorry if you thought we had a date this evening. I really am."

Mike's face mirrored a smug satisfaction when Jeff, without saying another word, walked away and disappeared into the elevator. Meredith, not failing to note Mike's expression, was immediately troubled by what had happened. This was more than just a conflict over her. She realized that now, although what it was or how long it had existed remained a mystery.

All through dinner Meredith's thoughts drifted

back to the encounter between the two men. The vindictive expression on Mike's face had taken her completely by surprise. It mirrored a quality she would have sworn he hadn't possessed.

"Penny for your thoughts," Mike said, bringing her back into reality.

Meredith hesitated, but then, taking a deep breath, continued. "What's between you and Jeff? It's more than me, that I know."

"You're very perceptive."

"That also doesn't answer my question."

"Meredith, the trouble between Jeff and myself goes back a long ways. I don't want to discuss it."

The air of finality and his icy tone made her realize that it wasn't likely she'd ever get an answer. Still, she made a mental note to keep her eyes and ears open.

After they completed their meal, Meredith asked to be taken back to the hotel.

"Jeff spoil the evening for you?"

"No, that's not it. I've got to go over some reports this evening. The aircraft is being taken up tomorrow. I want to make sure everything is ready and that there aren't any snags. I've put quite a few problems through the computer, and now I've got to analyze the data it gave back to me. There may be some last-minute things to fix, and I have to know exactly what those are before I go in tomorrow. Do you mind terribly?"

"Not at all. In fact, since I'm flying one of those birds, I think that's an excellent idea."

Meredith smiled. "Now that we agree on that, shall we go?"

True to his word, Mike drove her back, then escorted her to the room. When Meredith opened the door, the colorful array of flowers caused Mike to smirk. "Don't tell me. Someone died."

"Cute."

"Who's your admirer? Jeff?"

Meredith replied by giving him a cold stare. "I'm beginning to get just a bit fed up with people always wanting to know my business."

Mike, pulling her toward him, spoke softly. "I'm sorry, Meri. I didn't mean to make you angry."

"That's all right," Meredith replied with half a smile.

Mike leaned over, but instinctively Meredith turned her head. Kissing her on the cheek, Mike released her and took a step backward. "Angry still?"

"No, Mike. I just don't want you to get the wrong idea."

"You and Jeff?"

"No! Why does it always have to be someone else? I just don't want any commitments. All I have to offer is friendship. Take it or leave it."

"That's all I'm asking of you, Meri," Mike said softly. Touching the side of her face with a gentle caress, he added, "If you think I'm trying to rush you, then I apologize."

"Oh, Mike, I'm sorry! I didn't mean to snap at you! It's just been a pretty mixed-up day for me."

"I'll let you get back to work. I'll see you tomorrow."

Meredith walked inside, threw her purse on the chair, then sank on the edge of the bed dejectedly. What was wrong with her? Mike was the sweetest man in the world, yet she didn't feel drawn to him. Instead of the electricity or passion Jeff aroused in her, being with Mike elicited nothing more than a vague feeling of comfort. Despite her efforts, she couldn't get Jeff out of her mind. His hands, gentle and powerful, were tender in their caresses, as if he feared she would break under his touch. The strength of his masculinity and the fire of his kisses had woven a spell around her.

No! This was ridiculous. She was mixing up animal passions with love. Although the two were easily confused, they were in reality worlds apart. Besides, Jeff and she weren't right for each other. It was best to forget him. Still, the memory of the love they had shared, for a brief moment in time, burned in her mind... and in her body—as a promise of so much to come!

# - *5* -

FOUR WEEKS HAD passed since the emotionally charged
encounter with Jeff. Meredith had been working long,
exhausting hours to accommodate new deadlines. The
contractor involved with the radar system had hit a
few snags and had asked for extra time, but the Pen-
tagon had issued orders that the new aircraft was to
be either selected or scrapped in exactly three months.
Most of the major testing had not been done. Problems
with radar and weapons delivery had robbed her of
time needed to implement design changes. All of her
time was either spent with the Scorpio or working on
some aspect of it.

Under constant pressure, she had refused both Jeff
and Mike repeatedly as they continued to ask her to
lunch or dinner, trying to encroach on what little time
she called her own. Her persistent refusals had made
both men sulky and morose around her. Tensions
mounted with each passing day as rumors of dissen-

sion between Mike and Jeff circulated freely among
the staff.

The fighter, due for another test run this morning,
seemed to be in mint condition. Meredith had checked
and double-checked the system that had sabotaged the
first trial. Today she felt certain all would go according to schedule. Concerned over Jeff's safety, she
poured over computer printouts, studying each detail.

When the planes were taken from the hangar into
the bright sunlight, Meredith uttered a silent prayer.
Today the Scorpio would be tested for performance
in a catapult launch, the kind of takeoff it would use
on a carrier. Here, on base, they would get an idea
of what to expect, before it was actually tested at sea.

Meredith, standing inside the tower, saw Jeff come
from the hangar and walk toward the aircraft. He was
wearing the squadron's special uniform. She could
hear her heart beat like a drum in her ears as he crossed
the runway in his best military style. Before climbing
aboard the fighter, Jeff turned and gave her a snappy
salute. He was so confident and handsome! Meredith
scarcely breathed as she waited for the tests to begin.

Observing every detail with great care, she watched
the crew attach the Scorpio to the steam-pressured
catapult anchored in the concrete. Men moved away.
The pressure machinery below jerked the Scorpio
closer to the ground. Receiving the go-ahead signal
from the pilot, the technician on her right pulled a
lever. The fighter shot out like a bullet, but before
becoming completely airborne it dipped toward the
ground. Meredith's heart stopped for an eternity before the plane pulled back up. Holding her stomach,
she leaned against the wall. Oh God, she prayed silently, don't let anything happen to him. If she had
to fall in love again, why couldn't it have been with
a plumber? Realizing what she had just admitted, she
closed her eyes momentarily. When would she learn

that passion does *not* amount to love?

The fighter had just begun a circular pattern above the field when the raspy sounds of the radio jarred her.

*"Scorpio One* to Tower. Do you copy?"

"Read you loud and clear, *Scorpio One."*

"Experienced a power loss during takeoff. Shall I proceed with the testing as scheduled?"

Meredith shook her head, then glanced at the Navy engineers standing next to her. "To ensure maximum safety, we should have him come down," she said.

The plane captain agreed and gave the order, which the ensign relayed by radio. "Negative. That's negative, Commander Ryan. Return to base immediately."

Meredith was the first person out on the runway. "What happened?" she shouted to Jeff as he emerged from the cockpit.

"I lost power and then I saw the concrete coming up to greet me. I thought you said this plane was in shape!"

Hurt by his tone and the accusation he had leveled, Meredith felt her hackles rise. "I'll put every system through the wringer, Commander," she snapped. "We'll see what happened."

As soon as the ground crew had towed the aircraft back inside the hangar, Meredith began to work. Engineers and technicians from the base worked with her. Hours passed quickly. After checking all the major circuits and hooking the computer to the minor ones, they discovered no sign of a faulty system. If there was nothing wrong with the aircraft, the only other possibility was pilot error.

Taking a deep breath, she walked to Jeff's office and knocked on the door. This was going to be a confrontation she fervently wished she could avoid.

Jeff looked up from his desk and smiled. "What's up, beautiful? It's been an awful long time since you came here for a visit."

"Jeff, it's about the Scorpio," Meredith paused. With grim determination, she continued, "I've been over every component that could have had something to do with power loss during takeoff. Your people have gone over all the systems, checking and recheck-ing my work, and no one has been able to find the slightest indication of a malfunction."

Jeff clenched his fist, and his lips clamped into a thin hard line. It seemed an eternity before he spoke. "Listen, Meredith, I know my job. You must have made a mistake."

Meredith's eyes locked with his. "Jeff, it's not only my opinion. Navy engineers have been over that pro-totype with a fine-toothed comb. I'm telling you if there was a system's malfunction, it would have been spotted."

"And I'm telling you to go back downstairs and find the problem. I know with 100 percent certainty it was not pilot error. Just because you can't find out what went wrong, don't blame it on me."

Meredith's stance was casual, but the red tinge on her cheeks betrayed her emotion. "All right, hot shot. Let's just see what Scorpio does or doesn't do when *I* take it up."

"Over my dead body."

"That can be arranged."

"You haven't got the authorization." Jeff was standing now, glaring at her.

"The heck I haven't. Take a good look at the con-tract. It specifies I am authorized to take whatever steps I deem necessary to correct any problem. In this case, I've got to take her up."

"How many hours do you have in a high-performance aircraft like the Scorpio?"

"Not many."

"Exactly how many?"

"None, but I've flown other aircraft!"

"You'll get killed. You have no idea what it entails."

Meredith smiled, but her eyes held an icy glow. "All right. I concede. You're right, in this case."

"Thank God!"

"I'll have Mike take her up," she added hastily. "I'll ride in the navigator's seat."

He walked slowly toward her, stopping only inches away. "What Mike does or doesn't do is his own business, however, I'd hate to see you splattered all over the concrete. I'm a better pilot than Mike is. If I couldn't compensate for the loss of power, there's no way he can. You'll crash."

"I disagree," Meredith said flatly.

"Meri, don't do it," he growled.

She stared up at him, then spun on her heel. Jeff grabbed her arm and whirled her back around to face him.

"Let go of me," she demanded in a hard, impatient voice.

Jeff's mouth tightened. "If you insist on this, then I'll take her up."

"No. This is my decision to make, Commander, and I say Mike takes her up."

"I can't let you do that."

"Tough."

"All right then. Mike can take her up. Let me ride in the navigator's seat. I'm not sure how much help I can be from that position, but maybe I can keep him from crashing."

"I have to go up, and Mike is taking her up. That's final. I don't need you to babysit me."

"Like hell you don't."

Meredith glared at him, then turned and left the room. She knew her job and she knew the Scorpio. She went to her office and called for Mike to come to the strip to take the fighter up. If Jeff thought he could blame his error on the prototype, he was sadly mistaken. She went quickly to the hangar.

"Take her back outside and get her ready to fly," she told the crew chief standing by the craft.

"Yes, ma'am. Is Commander Ryan taking her back up?"

"No. Lieutenant Commander Lockwood is."

The man stared at her, then turned toward his companion. With a shrug he calmly began to carry out her instructions. The hangar seemed to come alive with whispered voices. Finally one of the younger men voiced the question that had been on all their minds.

"I thought the lieutenant commander was testing only the trainer version. This is Commander Ryan's aircraft."

"Commander Ryan claims the Scorpio has a major technical fault. I've checked it and I don't agree. We'd like to get another pilot's input. Any more questions, ensign?"

"No, ma'am," the man said, edging away.

In the supply room Meredith found a pressurized flight suit small enough to fit her and changed into it. She calmly walked toward an officer in flight gear, his face partially obscured by the deep shadow made by the hangar. Jeff was nowhere to be seen. She was glad he had decided not to come. Things were awkward enough without having a critic study every move she made. Crew and officers crowded around the pilot as a checklist was read off. Meredith waited, not wishing to interrupt. Her lips pursed as her knuckles curled tightly around the helmet's strap. When she looked up, she found Jeff squarely in front of her.

He stared evenly into her eyes. Suited in his squadron's colors he looked singularly impressive. As the full weight of their confrontation dawned on her, she braced herself. Taking a deep breath, she glanced away briefly. Her attention was captured by Mike, who stood leaning against one of the doorways. He eyed her thoughtfully, waiting for the final outcome.

Meredith raised her eyes to Jeff. "Commander Ryan, I'm afraid there's been a mistake. I wanted Lieutenant Commander Lockwood to take her up. I need input from another pilot for my records."

"Lieutenant Commander Lockwood is assigned to fly only the trainer version. This one's my charge."

"Please don't make this more difficult than it already is. Both aircraft are two-seaters and identical in most respects. Lieutenant Commander Lockwood is qualified to fly this version of the Scorpio and you know it. This is my decision to make, sir, and I would appreciate your cooperation."

While Mike, standing behind them, waited for his orders, Meredith's eyes locked with Jeff's. In one fluid motion, Jeff spun around, nodded to Mike, and walked away.

Meredith breathed a sigh of relief. Walking toward the aircraft, she waited for Mike to gather his gear. When he appeared she smiled. "You ready?"

"Sure am."

Meredith placed her hand on his arm. "Mike, I don't want to force you. I've been through this aircraft several times and so have your Navy people. She's ready to fly. Will you take her up?"

"Can do."

Mike scrambled up the fighter and eased himself into the pilot's seat, but Meredith shook her head.

"I can't use the steps on the side to get in. Bring

me a ladder," she told the crew chief.

"If you can't use the equipment, maybe you should stick to your job and stop trying to compete with me." Jeff's voice, loud enough to be heard by everyone around, came from behind her.

"Can it, mister. My legs don't stretch that way, and I don't see any reason to kill myself."

The men carried in a metal ladder and braced it against the side of the plane so that Meredith could climb aboard. Fitting herself comfortably into the seat, she buckled the harness. The plane captain, used to helping the pilots strap in, reached for one of the straps and brought it down across her chest. With a jump, he released the strap and placed his hands in the air.

"Ma'am, I'm sorry! I just...well, I was going to..."

Seeing the man turn a vivid shade of red, Meredith smiled. "I know. The extra equipment gets in the way, doesn't it?"

Seeing her smile, the plane captain relaxed and chuckled. "Yes, ma'am. It sure does."

Completing her preparations, she glanced at Mike and saw he was already strapped and buckled. The crew chief stepped in front of the fighter and began a series of hand signals. Mike watched, then responded, testing each of the systems. Meredith plugged the microphone jack to her helmet and listened as Mike gave a series of readings to the tower. Reaching up, he lowered the canopy, then, with a casual thumbs-up gesture, began to taxi toward the catapult. Meredith felt her mouth go dry as the fighter stopped, locked on the hold-back bar, then jerked downward.

"Ready, Meri?" came the muffled voice from the speakers.

"Ready, Mike."

Meredith inhaled, then placed her chin to her chest. In an instant, like a bullet from a pistol, the fighter was airborne. Meredith inhaled deeply, trying to catch her breath. Although she had known what to expect, the sensation of being hit squarely in the stomach persisted.

Climbing rapidly, the Scorpio made a shallow turn and leveled off. It had been a perfect takeoff. Meredith smiled when Mike turned partially toward her and made a circle with his thumb and forefinger. The fighter was responding to the slightest pressure from the controls.

"Mike, put her through a 180-degree turn."

"Roger."

The fighter, without a sign of trouble, turned, then continued its flight path. "Want to put her through some simple tests?"

"Yes. Try a shallow dive, then level again."

Again, the fighter responded easily. "She flies like a dream, Meri."

"Okay. Try a steep climb to 5,000 feet, then level off."

"You sure?"

"I'm not going to pass out with a pressure suit, Mike. Do it."

"Yes, ma'am!"

As the fighter was put through a battery of performance tests, Meredith kept a constant watch on the gauges and continued to question Mike. Finding no trace of a malfunction, she smiled.

"Take her down, Mike. I'm through."

"Roger."

As the fighter taxied to a stop, Meredith unstrapped her helmet and waited for the ground crew to appear. Somehow, proving her point had not brought her the satisfaction she had anticipated. She had made Jeff lose face, and he needed the respect of his colleagues in order to command. Her point should have been made without causing him any embarrassment. She released

her seat belts and allowed the plane captain to help her
to the ground. Shaking her hair, which had been matted
down by the helmet, Meredith walked toward the sol-
itary figure who stood with his back to her.

"Jeff," Meredith called softly. "God, I'm sorry."

Facing her, Jeff's expression remained impassive.
"I'm telling you the truth. There's something wrong
with that aircraft. It lost power right after takeoff. Meredith, I didn't imagine it nor did I ease back on the throttle accidentally."

"Jeff, we just took it for a test ride. Nothing happened," she responded quietly.

"I'm aware of that, but do something for me. Keep
checking, please."

"All right. I promise."

Jeff turned away in a gesture that was meant to dis-
miss her. Meredith fought the impulse to reach out to
him. She had not meant to hurt him, but she hadn't been
given a choice. It had been imperative to ascertain
whether the malfunction had been pilot error or not.
Still, the look in Jeff's eyes had cut through her. Perhaps after awhile he would realize she had only been
doing her job, and would not hold it against her.

Meredith walked back to the hangar. One of the officers glanced up and came over to congratulate her on
the Scorpio's successful test run. Meredith nodded ab-
sently, her mind still on the man she had upstaged. Had
she done the right thing?

Working on reports connected to the test flight,
Meredith completely lost track of the time. Suddenly
aware she was hungry, she decided to make use of the
candy machine down the hall. As she neared the door
to the conference room, she heard laughter and loud
voices. She recognized the captain's voice.

"You must be getting old and loosing your touch,
Jeff. Ready to give up your wings, yet?"

As the officers continued to tease him, Meredith felt

her heart ache. Debating whether to go to his defense, she stood immobile. Realizing it was better to let him handle the situation, she turned away. Tears welling inside her eyes, she sought refuge in the ladies' restroom. After a few minutes she wiped the tears away and returned to work.

Just before quitting time, Jeff came to her office. Meredith, immediately aware of his presence, stopped and glanced expectantly at him.

"Did you check the aircraft?"

"Not yet. I've been working on these reports, but I'll put the fighter through every test I can think of tomorrow. I told you I would, and I'll keep my word."

Nodding silently, Jeff started to leave. Before he stepped out, Meredith sprang from her chair and went to his side. "Jeff, share dinner with me tonight. My treat. We'll make it a picnic."

"Meredith, you don't have to feel sorry for me. There is something wrong with the Scorpio. Besides, if you think I need your pity, you're sadly mistaken."

"Jeff, it isn't like that at all!"

"Isn't it!" Jeff spun around abruptly and strode out, leaving Meredith hurt and bewildered. Walking back to her desk, she picked up her things and prepared to leave. As she was going out the door, Mike sauntered by.

"Hey, that was some fancy flying we did today."

Meredith remained silent and pretended to concentrate on locking her door.

"Anytime you want to fly with me, just say the word."

"I appreciate your confidence, Mike. I'm glad you took her up and that the tests went so well, but this type of thing is a rare occurrence. I just had to find out for myself what, if anything, was going haywire with the Scorpio."

Overlooking the weariness in her voice, Mike pressed on. "How about dinner tonight. I'll help you celebrate."

Anger exploded inside her and she turned to face him. "Listen, Mike, I did what I had to do, but I've hurt a nice guy in the process. I'm not pleased or proud of that."

"Meredith, I'm sorry. I had no idea . . ."

"I heard the guys razzing him, and I think the way they're treating him is perfectly awful."

"If the shoes were reversed, he'd do it to us."

"Maybe, but it's still a crummy thing to do."

"Okay. I'll tell you what. Let me pick you up at seven and I won't say another word."

"Mike, I can't. I'm in an awful mood. All I really want to do is go to bed."

"Now, come on. You still have to eat."

"I was planning to have a glass of milk and a candy bar."

"That's not a proper meal."

"I said no."

Hearing the sharp edge in her voice, Mike shrugged and walked away. Now why couldn't she have been civil to him? What was happening to her? Ever since she had taken the job at the test site things had not gone right. Today she had even managed to demoralize the man whose respect she valued the most. Swallowing the bitterness at the back of her throat, Meredith drove back to the hotel. Once inside her room, she hurled her briefcase on the bed. It had been a thoroughly rotten day. Perhaps after a few days had passed it would all be forgotten.

There was a slim chance she could find something wrong with the Scorpio, something that would prove Jeff's claim and thus vindicate him. But what? She was certain there was nothing wrong, and she couldn't fabricate a problem. Others would be called in to verify any malfunction.

Well, perhaps Jeff was right. Tomorrow she would pull the Scorpio apart bolt by bolt. If there was anything there, she'd find it.

# - 6 -

THE NEXT MORNING Meredith carefully ran all the systems through a meticulous computer check. Finding nothing, she turned to the mechanics for the solution. The men diligently checked the aircraft, and after several hours no sign of trouble could be found. Meredith returned to the upstairs office, slammed the door shut, then kicked the metal cabinet by her desk.

With a yelp of pain, she retreated from the object, holding her foot. "Swine file!"

Crossing to her desk she sat down. How could she tell Jeff? Surely there was some way to say this without muddling things up or wrecking his confidence!

Hearing a knock on her door, Meredith looked up, but before she had a chance to respond, Jeff burst inside. Standing ramrod stiff he kept his voice unnaturally steady.

"Let's have it."

"Jeff, your mechanics and engineers checked, I checked, the computer checked..."

"Nothing? No one found anything?"

"I'm really sorry, Jeff. I truly wish I could have said something was wrong with the Scorpio."

"So you still think it was me."

"Jeff, stop. I can't change things and God knows I can't stand it when you look at me that way!"

Smiling ruefully, Jeff turned and left the room. Meredith didn't have much of an appetite, but she needed to get out of the base. She needed a distraction that would take her mind off the events there. Picking up her purse, she almost ran to her car. Once on the freeway, she pressed down hard on the accelerator. After about thirty minutes, she stopped at a hamburger stand. The French fries were greasy and the hamburger had not been thoroughly cooked, but nothing seemed to matter. The food was tasteless in her mouth. Wiping her hands, she deposited the remains in the trash container, then began to drive back to the base.

Meredith parked her small compact and reluctantly prepared to go inside. As she walked toward the hangar, her attention was diverted. Her eyes grew wide as she realized what was happening. The Scorpio was on the runway, poised over the catapult, ready to launch. Running over to the area, she positioned herself in a spot where she could observe things clearly. He was a good pilot. Whatever had caused him before to pull back on the throttle wouldn't be repeated. With a smile, she waited for that perfect textbook launch.

The aircraft, released from the catapult, lurched forward at incredible speed. Meredith could hear the engines loose power. The fighter seemed to hang motionless a few hundred feet from the ground, clawing desperately at the air. Bracing herself for the impact, she stared, unable to move.

Jeff knew there was no time to think. Reacting with the instincts of an experienced pilot, he lit the afterburners, pushing the fighter to its very limits. He needed more speed, or a miracle, to remain airborne.

Slowly the Scorpio responded, struggling toward the sky. Only a few seconds had elapsed since takeoff, yet in those brief moments he had come face to face with death. Once again, the victory had been his.

Meredith swallowed, trying to keep down the contents of her stomach. Jeff had been right. There had been no mistaking it. The engines had almost stopped in midair. Fighting the nausea that threatened to overcome her, Meredith waited as the Scorpio taxied down the runway.

Technicians and ground crew crowded around the Scorpio like moths around a light. Even though he had obviously scheduled the flight without her knowledge, she felt no bitterness toward him. Meredith strained for a view of the pilot, but was unable to catch even a glimpse. People shouted questions, inquiring about fluid levels and responses from control mechanisms; Jeff tried to answer them as quickly as possible. Ground crew hooked the aircraft to the tractor, seemingly oblivious to the chaos around them. As soon as Jeff climbed down, they started to tow the fighter back into the hangar.

As the ground crew and engineers followed the disabled aircraft inside, Jeff spotted Meredith. He pulled her roughly to the side of the tower, away from prying eyes.

"Don't tell me that was my fault, or I swear I'll wring your neck!"

"No, Jeff. You were right. I heard the engines myself. I don't have a clue, but it wasn't your fault." Meredith felt a tear spill down her cheek; she quickly turned and wiped it away.

Jeff, noticing it, immediately softened his tone. "Meri, I'm sorry. It's just that the last few days have been hell."

"You could have been killed! I never really considered the possibility you could have been right. I would never do anything to purposely hurt you, yet my negligence almost cost you your life!" Meredith's voice broke. Swallowing convulsively, she tried to fight the tears stinging her eyes.

Jeff brought her against him, holding on to her tightly. His lips brushed her forehead while he stroked her hair tenderly. "It wasn't your fault. A lot of people certified that fighter safe too."

Meredith looked at him, then, drawing strength from his words, wrapped her arms around him. Jeff, responding instinctively to her needs, leaned down and parted her lips with his tongue, exploring the sweetness of her mouth. Meredith yielded as a warmth spread through her. A sigh escaped her lips as she clung to him, afraid to let him go.

Slowly Jeff pushed her back. "You are mine, Meri. When will you finally see that and accept it?"

Suddenly aware of what she had done, Meredith stepped back. Her voice cracked into a falsetto as she fought a momentary feeling of panic. "Jeff, I got carried away. This doesn't mean . . . well, you shouldn't think . . ."

"Meri, why do you fight what your heart tells you every time we're together? We're so right together."

"No. It's passion you stir in me, Jeff, and that isn't love, don't you see?"

"A passion borne of love, maybe, Meri. Give us a try. If you don't, we may both get hurt."

"No! I don't know what you're talking about," she blurted, then ran toward the hangar.

She was hardly ready to face the others when she reached the hangar. The news had spread quickly. A group of Navy engineers who had overseen the testing came toward her immediately.

"No, gentlemen, I have no idea what happened. You know as well as I do that the aircraft checked out fine. Yet, when that fighter took off I heard the engine speed drop and almost stall. There *is* something wrong with one of the systems and we've got to find out what." Looking at the perplexed faces around her, she added, "Don't ask me how. If anyone has any suggestions, I'd love to hear them."

When no one spoke up, Meredith spread her hands in the air in a gesture of helplessness. "We'll have to come up with something. It's either a malfunction or a design problem in one of the components. I'm going to make a direct link with our computer in Carmel and feed it all the information we have on the Scorpio's tests. Let's see what solutions it offers."

She turned away, prepared to double her efforts in an attempt to find the elusive malfunction. If Jeff had died, she would have been responsible. She had refused to listen, and then had caused those miserable morons to tease him unmercifully. Meredith looked at the papers verifying the checks made before flight. She had covered everything, yet she was obviously overlooking something. All further test flying would have to be postponed until she found the cause of the malfunction. There would be no other lives risked.

Many hours were spent trying to figure out the problem, but every conceivable test turned out negative. As a final effort, Meredith arranged to have the trainer prototype placed side by side with the one she was working on. They would check the systems against one another. Maybe something would turn up.

The rest of the week passed quickly as Meredith, unable to find the problem, requested that engineers from the factory come and help. Time passed slowly as they programmed the computer for new analytical data.

Friday, as Meredith sat alone on her desk eating a sandwich, Jeff sauntered into her office.

"How's my lady?"

"In a very crabby mood, and I'm not your lady."

"Oh, yes you *are* my lady." He chuckled softly. "My crabby lady. Listen, I have a terrific idea."

"Spare me. I'd rather feel sorry for myself."

"Come away with me for the weekend."

"You've lost your mind."

"Come on. It would be fun." Jeff's eyes twinkled mischievously as he continued to pressure her. "Besides, you need a rest."

"The last thing you'd give me would be a rest, Jeff Ryan."

"I promise I'll be an absolute pussycat all weekend. Really I've—"

"Jeff! I'm tired. I've worked twelve hours a day this past week, and this weekend is all mine. I'm not, I repeat, *not* going to share it with anyone."

Jeff looked at her pensively, concern mirrored in his eyes. Noting it, Meredith smiled.

"I'm okay, Jeff. It's just that after a week like this one, I've got to get away and forget all about business."

"I think I can help you do that rather well."

"No. Besides, I've made other plans."

"With Mike?" Jeff's words were harsh and cold.

"If it's any of your business, no, not with Mike. I told you. I need time for myself."

Jeff shrugged. "Have it your way."

Meredith watched him leave. It would be much easier if he'd just give up, she concluded. Why couldn't he accept her decision? She would never be able to trust another man again, and trust was something that she knew went hand in hand with love. Besides, her feelings for him had little to do with love—at least the kind that would last a lifetime. Yet she couldn't deny he had become ever present in her thoughts. Whenever he was in a room, he seemed to overshadow the men around him by sheer force of presence. His irrepressible smile and his special charisma affected her more than she cared to admit.

Meredith threw her pencil down on the desk and strode out of the small office. She would get a cup of coffee and relax, even if it was only for a few minutes. Walking to the coffee machine down the hall, she dropped her coins into the slot, then glanced at the selection of candy bars in the other machine. Without looking, she reached for the Styrofoam cup, but the machine had malfunctioned: steaming coffee poured over her hand. She cried out and jerked her hand back.

"Rats!" she yelled, kicking the side of the machine.

Bill, the backup test pilot, peered out of the doorway and glanced down the hall. Realizing what had occurred, he began to laugh.

"You laugh when that stupid thing just about cooked my hand?" Meredith asked through clenched teeth.

"That'll teach you not to look."

"Boy, you're really a bundle of sympathy."

Bill smiled apologetically. "Okay, let's look at your hand."

"See? It's turning red."

"Poor baby!"

Meredith scowled. "That's some comfort you give the wounded! Is there a first-aid kit around here?"

Bill led the way to a small supply room. He got a tube of salve from a box and handed it to her. Meredith dabbed a little on and soothed it over her painful skin.

"Thanks," she said, tossing the tube to him. "You're taller, so you get to put it back."

"Oh, but then you'll become dependent on me."

"I thought that's what all you macho types wanted."

"Not me." Tossing it back to her, he added, "Put it back yourself."

"You'd make a delicate, wounded creature like me work?"

"Sure. That's what us macho dudes do best, didn't you know?"

Seeing Meredith's face, Bill laughed. "All right. I'll put it away. I'll place the box lower so the clumsier types around here can reach it more easily."

Meredith grinned. "Thank you, sir."

Together they walked back to the other end of the hall. "I hear you've been having a pretty miserable week," he said.

"That's the understatement of the year!"

"Look, Betsy and I had planned to spend the weekend at a mountain cabin owned by one of the guys, but now our little girl has flu so we can't go. Why don't you use it? It's up around Lake Arrowhead. I hear it's beautiful there this time of year."

"You're not going to use it? Really? I'd love it. It sounds terrific.

"All yours," Bill said. He pulled out a set of keys from his pocket, opened the key chain, and extracted the right one. "I'll give you the map I have that shows how to get there. The cabin is hidden from view. You won't be able to see it until you're right there!"

"Will I need a four-wheel-drive vehicle?"

"No. There's supposed to be a gravel road that leads almost to the cabin. The trick is finding that little road. Apparently, from the main road it's really easy to miss."

After explaining the map and giving her all the directions he could think of, Bill wished her good luck.

"Thanks! I was planning to go off by myself, and this is just what I needed. I'm sorry about your little girl, though."

"That's okay. It comes with the territory, you know."

Meredith had shopped after work and stuffed the little cooler she had purchased to the rim. Making sure she had an ample supply of fresh water, she began the long drive. With the radio turned on, she soon became absorbed in the music and the passing scenery. Pines and cedars dotted the landscape, adding a richness of color to the blanket of green that surrounded her. Off in the distance, snow-capped mountains towered majestically over the horizon. The air grew crisp as the little car accelerated, climbing into the heart of the mountain range. As she continued, carefully decreasing her speed when approaching each curve or turn in the road, she began to keep a sharp lookout for the cutoff Bill had mentioned. Suddenly, she spotted it. Almost obscured by the vegetation surrounding it was a narrow and unpaved road. Shifting to a lower gear, she proceeded slowly. Daylight had already begun to fade and she was eager to arrive. Looking around, she searched for any sign of the cabin but could see only wilderness. Soon, she began to wonder if she had taken the wrong road. As she reached the top of an incline, though, she spotted it.

The small vacation home could barely be called a cabin. She had been expecting a wooden-log type like the one on the syrup bottles, but what she had here was a beautiful home that happened to have been built out of logs.

Spacious yet still retaining its rustic charm, the vacation home was immaculately clean. The kitchen, directly to the left of the front door, was small but contained all the modern amenities. Pleasantly surprised, Meredith decided to take a look before organizing her things.

The livingroom had a huge fireplace nestled in the

corner. Alongside were neatly stacked logs. Down the long corridor, to Meredith's delight, was a small bathroom, which meant she'd be spared sojourns to an outhouse!

She went to the kitchen, opened a can of soup, and prepared it on the stove. After eating the soup and a couple of pieces of toast, she decided to go for a short walk. A sudden storm blew in and she had to race back, arriving soaked and cold. After making sure the door was locked, she made a fire, stripped off her wet clothes, and laid them to dry on a chair. Fishing a warm robe from her suitcase, she wrapped the familiar garment around her snugly, then built a fire. A flash of lightning illuminated the cabin, followed by a slow rolling thunder that seemed to shake the foundation of the house. Meredith sat up startled. The lights flickered momentarily, then went out. Good thing she had not expected anything modern. Exhausted from the long drive, she stretched out on the couch.

Meredith turned in her sleep, but then, feeling constricted, woke. Opening her eyes slowly, she tried to stretch. The robe had wrapped tightly around her and refused to give way. Too sleepy to find pajamas, she slipped the robe completely off, setting it down beneath her.

She took a blanket tossed over a small couch and covered herself with it. The blanket and the fire would keep her warm. How lovely to be alone, miles from anyone! Snuggling deep into the blanket, she began to feel groggy, but instantly became alert at the faint creaking of footsteps on the wooden floor. Feigning sleep, she listened for sounds, trying to determine the exact location of the intruder. All of a sudden an icy hand was upon her shoulder. Meredith moved quickly, prepared to fight to protect herself. Then she gasped.

"Jeff! What are you doing here?"

Jeff smiled and cocked his head. "You're too distracting that way. I think you better pull the blanket over yourself."

Realizing she was completely naked, Meredith yanked the blanket over her breasts, exposing the lower portion of her body. When Jeff's eyes slid downward, Meredith tried to stretch the blanket for more coverage. "Get out of here!"

"I can't, sweetheart, even if I wanted to, which I don't. My car got stuck in the mud half way up the last hill and I had to hike the rest of the way."

"At least turn around while I wrap the robe around myself."

"Why? I've already seen everything."

"Jeff, now!" Meredith screamed.

Complying, he turned away from her. "You are really a beautiful woman, Meri."

She ignored his compliment. "One of us is leaving. If you insist on staying, then I'm going."

"You can't. The road is completely washed out. Look for yourself if you don't believe me. It's a mess. You'll only get stuck."

Meredith glanced out the window. Unable to see anything, she got a flashlight and went to the door. The beam revealed a river of mud with leaves floating on the surface where the path had been. "What are we going to do? I only have enough supplies for the weekend."

Jeff led her into the kitchen. "I brought a few things too. Don't worry. I'll take care of both of us."

"Wonderful!" Meredith replied, sarcasm dripping with every syllable.

"We're stuck, Meri. You might as well learn to make the best of it."

"All right. I'll take the bed. You can sleep out here."

"Think again."

Exploding with fury, Meredith turned to face him.

Her eyes blazed as they bored right through him. Instead of feeling uncomfortable, Jeff smiled.

"The bed's a mess, kiddo. There's a leak in the roof. All your things and the mattress are soaked beyond hope. Go see for yourself."

Meredith, with the robe wrapped tightly around her, strode down the hall. The bed and all her clothing were hopelessly waterlogged.

"Why me?" Meredith moaned.

Jeff came up from behind her and leaned casually against the wall. "Don't worry. It's all right. You're safe with me."

"Some choice. Either I leave and drown out there, or I can stay here with you. All I wanted was a serene weekend."

Jeff reached for her chin, tilting her face toward him. His eyes glinted with mockery. "Serenity went out the window when I walked in the door, huh?"

She nodded curtly and stepped into the bedroom. She retrieved her wet clothes, pushed past Jeff who chuckled at her stiff back, and went to the bathroom. She rinsed the clothes and carried them to the fire. Her other clothes, she noted gratefully, had almost dried. She was spreading out her wet things, when Jeff spoke.

"I've got some groceries in the car. As soon as it's daylight, I'll go out and get them. For tonight, we'll use yours."

"I've already eaten, so help yourself. You can't cook anything. The electricity is out, so you'll have to rough it."

"When the fire starts to die down, I'll warm a can of something in the coals."

"Thank God we've got plenty of wood. I'd hate to think of being trapped here without any heat."

"We'd think of something."

"I know it's hard, darling, but do try to divert that one-track mind of yours!"

"Meredith, are you really bound and determined to make an already impossible situation worse?"

"I certainly didn't invite you up here. By the way, how did you get the use of the cabin for this particular weekend?"

Jeff's eyes mirrored amusement as he answered, "Sweetheart, I own half of this place."

Meredith looked away with a gesture of sheer disgust.

"Actually, this is a very romantic setting, don't you agree?" Jeff asked in a teasing tone.

"Yes. Too bad Mike isn't here."

Her answer brought the expected response. Jeff's eyes became cold and hard. As his hand clenched, Meredith wondered if she had gone too far. Jeff stared evenly at her, then walked into the kitchen.

Breathing a silent sigh of relief, she sat down close to the fire. Why couldn't they be civil? Every time they were around each other lately it was impossible to keep from having five quick rounds.

Jeff selected a can of pork and beans, then began to eat from it. Sitting at the table across the room, he kept his eyes on the window, even though the darkness prevented him from seeing outside. Silence hung heavy between them.

Meredith felt trapped in an atmosphere of helplessness. She was completely at the mercy of forces she could not control. The weather had brought them together, forcing a confrontation she had hoped to avoid. She was aware of his efforts not to look at her, or even in her direction. Stung by the rejection, yet knowing full well she had caused it, Meredith stared blankly into the fire.

"Jeff, I'm sorry. I didn't mean it the way it sounded."

"Meri, I know exactly what you're doing, but don't ever throw his name at me that way again."

Meredith's eyes met his. The intensity of his voice

had surprised her. What could have caused such a rift between the two of them? "Why do you hate each other?"

"Meredith, Mike is my enemy. He would do anything in his power to hurt me."

"Mike wouldn't do anything of the sort. He's a very gentle person."

"Believe me when I tell you he has another side— one he's chosen to keep hidden from you. Let's not talk about him anymore, all right?"

Meredith shrugged, then glanced at her watch. "It's very, very late. What do you say we get some sleep."

"Good idea. I'm bushed."

"Do you have a blanket?"

"In the car."

"It won't do you much good there, will it? I have an extra one you can use. It's inside my suitcase," she said, then added, ". . . wet."

"That's okay. I'll keep my jacket on.

"Didn't you bring any blankets or clothing with you?"

"All I brought was a small pack under my jacket. It was too wet and cold out there, and I had to hike quite a ways."

Meredith remained silent for a minute. "Look, you'll freeze. Come sit by the fire. We can share my blanket."

Jeff's eyes softened. "Are you sure you trust me?"

"You'll keep your word."

As he lay next to her, Meredith pushed her pillow to the middle. "We might as well share this too."

Meredith rolled on her side, facing away from him. After a few minutes she felt him toss the covers aside and sit up. Turning around, she noticed he was unbuttoning his shirt.

"What are you doing?"

"I'm just going to take my shirt off. You don't

mind, do you? It's warmer than I thought so close to the fire."

"I'm comfortable, but if you'd like we can move back a little bit."

"No, I'll be all right as soon as I take this off. The flannel was beginning to stick to me."

Meredith watched him walk across the room and toss his shirt on the chair. As he came closer, she could feel her body tingle with desire. It was no use trying to ignore the response his virility aroused in her. Meredith watched him as he stirred the ashes in the fireplace and placed a fresh log in the flames. His bronzed torso glistened against the flickering light. An overwhelming ache pulsed through her. She wanted him, and despite her efforts to the contrary, she did love him. Still she found it difficult to give him her trust. Deep down she feared he would use her then discard her when he tired of her. Meredith shut her eyes, trying to withdraw into herself. When he stooped down, ready to share the warmth of the blanket, she turned away.

"Meri, why are you so afraid of me?"

Meredith remained still, hardly breathing. Perhaps if she didn't respond, he wouldn't press her. Biting her lower lips, she waited.

Jeff reached over and turned her toward him. "Look at me, baby."

Meredith trembled slightly as the emotions she had ardently denied surfaced. Her eyes seemed abnormally large against the paleness of her skin. Her mouth curled in an unnatural smile and she shook her head, not daring to trust her voice.

Jeff caressed her cheek lightly. "Meri, what am I going to do with you?"

Sensing her response, Jeff edged closer to her. Slowly he pulled her head toward his descending lips. The fire of his kiss caused a weakness to spread over her. His hands felt rough against the smoothness of his flesh. Passion leaped between them like a living flame as his tongue slid between her eager lips, tasting the moist sweetness there. His hand slipped easily between the folds of the robe, molding and kneading the soft flesh trapped inside. Meredith twisted away from him, trying to regain a measure of self-control, but his arms held her against him. Feeling his hardness press against her, Meredith arched toward him, moaning softly. An all-consuming ache grew between them as they explored the depths of their need.

"Jeff," she sighed, every nerve in her body alive.

As he pulled away from her to catch his breath, Meredith studied the intensity in the ruggedly handsome face. His eyes seemed alive with the current of emotions passing between them, yet there was an undefinable gentleness in them. Mirrored in his face was a compelling look that made wildfire leap along her veins. His eyes gleamed with confidence in his own masculinity.

With tender persistence, he forced her back on the pillow. As his hands slid over the curve of her hips and felt the silky, pliant flesh, his kisses became harsh, demanding in their urgency. Undoing the knot in her bathrobe, he pulled the material away from her body, then pulled away. His eyes devoured every swell and curve.

"Jeff," she murmured, "love me."

"Are you truly ready to face your feelings for me?"

"Yes." Her lips quivered expectantly. "I am in love with you."

"I've known that all along, sweetheart." His face reflected a quiet tenderness.

Despite her urgings, Jeff would not be rushed. Resting his head on one hand, he caressed the gentle contours of her body, then leaned over her, kissing her hard and possessively. Matching his intensity,

Meredith felt him respond. Her hand ran over the rippling muscles of his back. With a new sureness, she caressed the hard flesh of his torso, then slipped her hand down, toward the core of his maleness.

With a sharp intake of breath, Jeff pushed her down until she rested on her back. Gentleness left him as a savage passion overpowered every nerve in his body. Kissing her harshly, he left her lips throbbing and red. Meredith shuddered convulsively as his mouth slid down her cheeks to the base of her throat. His tongue left a trail of fire as it lingered by her breasts, teasing the honey-brown peaks. Sensation after sensation rippled through her as she gave herself to the magic of his touch. His hands dug into the smooth roundness of her buttocks as he shifted, positioning her beneath him with his expert hands. Senses reeling, they merged into one joyously throbbing entity.

Sunlight streamed through the window, nudging her awake. Meredith rubbed her eyes and turned away from the harsh light. Picking up her dried clothing from the chair, she went to the small bathroom and dressed. Jeff was nowhere in sight. Worried, she stepped outside and glanced down the road. His car was still there.

Meredith fixed a simple breakfast consisting of toast and a bit of cereal, and ate more out of habit than hunger. After she finished, she opened the door and looked around. The ground had begun to firm up, and it looked as if by Sunday they would be able to leave easily.

Seeing Jeff walking down the road, boots covered with mud, Meredith waved. It was no use trying to deny it. She loved Jeff more than she had dreamed possible. The feelings that had existed between her and Mark would never compare to those she shared with Jeff. She knew now; they belonged together.

As he neared, Meredith looped her arm around his, squeezing it gently. "Good morning."

Jeff smiled. "Good morning, yourself. It looks like we won't be trapped here much longer."

"I know. Isn't it a pity."

Jeff grinned. "You know I love you, don't you?"

"Uh huh, but it's nice to hear."

Sweeping her into his arms, he held her close to him. Meredith rested her head on his shoulders. Enticed by the sweetness of the scent she wore, Jeff pressed her a little tighter. "Meri, I've been waiting for a long time for you to admit to yourself you're in love with me."

"I do love you."

"I knew it." His mouth curled in an arrogant grin.

Meredith and Jeff spent the morning talking and loving. The bright sun had hardened the roads and, eager to explore the area around the cabin, they decided to go for a walk. The smell of the woods and the freshness of the air were exhilarating. Meredith, contented, kept her hand snuggled inside Jeff's.

As they approached the lake, Meredith looked around. She walked toward a log and sat down, motioning for him to join her. Jeff shook his head and paced for a few minutes. Meredith, perplexed, watched him but said nothing.

Stopping in mid stride, directly in front of her, Jeff looked into her eyes. "Meri, will you marry me?"

Meredith swallowed, aware of the dryness in her throat. "Did you just say what I thought you said?"

"I asked you to be my wife."

She gasped, jumped to her feet, and flung her arms around him. "Yes. I want that more than anything else in this world."

Jeff laughed. "Then it's settled. We'll wait until the testing is over, then we'll have time to come back here and have a proper honeymoon." Pulling her toward him, he kissed her long and hard."

As the afternoon waned, they tidied up the cabin, readying it for its next occupant. Jeff helped Meredith load her equipment and supplies into her car. Once finished, he carried his pack down the road to his vehicle. After watching him for a few seconds, she called out to him.

"Wait! I have an idea. Just pile your stuff into my car and we'll drive to your car. It'll be easier and faster. What do you say?"

"Sounds good."

After making sure the cabin was safely locked up, Meredith started her car and eased it into low gear. She drove slowly, trying to avoid the muddier spots in the road. When they reached Jeff's Porsche, she helped him transfer his belongings, then returned to her car.

"I'll wait for you to pull out, then I'll follow you into town," she suggested.

"Okay."

Meredith felt sad as they left the mountain setting. Seeing him glance in his rear-view mirror, she smiled. Why had she fought him for so long? He was everything a woman could want in a man. She would now work twice as hard to finalize the testing.

The temperature grew decidedly warmer as they left the higher altitudes. Meredith, uncomfortable in the confines of the car, unzipped her jacket and lowered her window a few inches. The air still felt damp against her skin, but the breeze was refreshing. Shifting in her seat, she tried to relax and enjoy the trip. Mountains and valleys covered in a lush mantle of green stretched everywhere while snowcapped peaks towered majestically in the distance. Allowing herself only fleeting glances at the countryside, she kept her eyes on the road, concentrating on the highway ahead of her. As she tried to keep up with Jeff's car, Meredith felt vaguely disquieted. The trip to the cabin, although long, had not been unpleasant. Now the moments took forever to pass. Her stomach muscles cramped and a headache began to throb at the base of her neck.

Glancing at the speedometer, she uttered a loud oath. Her jaws clenched as she shook her head. Methodically, she slowed her car. Within minutes, she had lost sight of Jeff's car. Slowly and deliberately, she pulled to the side of the road and stopped. Reaching inside her glove compartment, she picked out her maps and set them on the seat beside her. Although well aware Jeff would soon turn back, she had no intention of driving the rest of the way at such a high speed. Ignoring his approach, she poured over her maps.

Jeff pulled his silver Porsche alongside her, then smiled. "What's the problem?"

"My mother didn't raise me to become a race-car driver."

"I wasn't going that fast!"

"Not for a bat out of hell," she responded sweetly.

"I thought you could handle it."

"I'm sorry. I just don't approve of suicide attempts on the highway. It could clog traffic, you know."

"I'll tell you what," Jeff responded with a grin. "You lead. I'll follow."

"Isn't that just like a man! Always needing a woman to show him the way."

Jeff turned his face away, mumbling something incoherent about braiding her lips. Taking a deep breath, he turned toward her again. "You tell me. What shall we do next?"

"You're more familiar with the area. Lead on, sir, but go slower, please."

"You got it."

As they neared the city, Meredith realized from

their route that Jeff was planning to stop by her hotel. Pleased, she smiled, then honked her horn. As he glanced in his rear-view mirror, she made a circle with her thumb and forefinger. Before long, they were both parked in the hotel's parking lot.

Jeff sauntered over to her car and helped unload and carry her provisions inside. "You're going to drive me crazy," he said, shaking his head.

"Don't worry. It'll be a short trip."

Meredith stopped in front of her door and sat down. As she sorted through her purse, searching for the room key, Jeff spun her around and kissed her thoroughly.

"I have business to take care of at the base tonight and tomorrow, but I'll call around five. We can have dinner together."

"All right."

"See you then," he said, giving her a quick kiss.

Meredith watched him walk down the corridor until he disappeared around the corner. What a man! She could have died of love for him at that minute.

## - 7 -

BY THE TIME Meredith awoke, the already hot sun
was streaming through her window. Looking forward
to a nice shopping expedition in the city, she dressed
casually in a tan corduroy blazer and black slacks.
When she left the hotel, she glanced at her watch and
realized that the morning had given way to the afternoon.

Time passed quickly as she explored store after
store, pricing everything from linens to appliances.
As she stopped by the counter of an exclusive shop,
Meredith glanced at the clock behind the register.
Verifying the time with her own wristwatch, she
dashed toward the car. Not wanting to miss Jeff's
call, she drove back to the hotel.

Munching on the only food she had eaten all day,
a candy bar, she began filling the tub. After bathing,
she carefully unwrapped one of her packages. Nestled
between the thin sheets of paper lay a pale blue dress.

The lightly knitted fabric would flatter her trim figure. She had spotted it in the window of one of the smaller boutiques and had fallen in love with it. Created in a repeating shell pattern, the heathery blue dress had a plunging neckline. Although it was a bit daring, the dress was so beautiful she had purchased it immediately.

She slipped it over her head and smoothed it over her body. It was lovely. The shade went well with her coloring, and the snug fit gave her a trim, sleek look. Searching for something to wear around her neck, she finally chose an Indian necklace composed of tiny gold beads interlaced with turquoise. It went with the dress beautifully. Putting on a pair of black suede heels, she spun in front of the mirror, pleased with her appearance.

When the telephone rang, Meredith verified the time Jeff would pick her up for dinner. She had not misunderstood. He had said six-thirty. It seemed odd; she knew he preferred to eat at a later hour. Shrugging, she smiled. At least she would get to see him that much sooner! Arranging her hair so it draped smoothly around her shoulders, Meredith sprayed a tiny bit of her favorite perfume behind each ear.

She glanced around the room and grimaced. What a mess! Quickly tossing boxes and wrappings underneath the bed, she smoothed the bedspread, making sure it draped to the floor. She had just finished, when the familiar knock sounded at the door. Smiling at his promptness, she opened the door and allowed him inside.

Jeff's eyes slid slowly down her figure, while Meredith, with a satisfied grin, allowed him to assess her.

"You look absolutely fantastic!" he said softly.

"Thank you."

Meredith had not failed to notice his appearance

either. The dark blue corduroy three-piece suit seemed
to bring out his eyes, accentuating his most appealing
feature.

Jeff closed the door behind him, then bringing her
close to him, whispered, "Come here."

Meredith yielded easily, snuggling deep into his
arms. Responding to his kiss, she knew yet again the
shocks of desire he could cause to quake through her
body. He released her, groaning, and looked at her
through half-opened lids. The slumberous passion was
in her eyes too. With obvious effort, he gained control
of himself.

"I've got a surprise for you," he said. "Hurry and
get your things."

Meredith picked up her purse. Handing him her
coat, she waited as he helped her put it on. "What
kind of surprise?"

"You'll see."

Meredith's eyes glowed with interest. Slowly an
infectious grin spread over her face. "That sounds
nifty! Let's go. I can't wait to see what it is."

Laughing, he placed his arm around her shoulders
protectively and escorted her to his car. Meredith
seemed to sparkle with happiness, a response that
delighted Jeff completely. After a short drive, he
turned the car into a crowded parking lot and stopped.
Directly in front of them was a busy pier filled with
a colorful assortment of pleasure craft.

"We're here."

"We're where?"

Jeff chuckled, then walked around the car and
helped her out. Reaching for her hand, he pulled her
along gently. "Come on, you'll love this."

Meredith looked around her quizzically as he continued to walk along the rustic water-darkened pier.
Finally, as they reached the end, she saw a long,

gleaming white yacht. On its polished wooden deck, near the stern, was a beautifully set table. A waiter, dressed in his best black and whites, stood waiting to welcome them aboard.

Eyes wide, Meredith grinned. "Is this for us?"

"Of course. This is the beginning of a very special night."

"You mean, there's more?"

"Wait and see."

Jeff stepped over to the deck, then turned to help her come aboard. Meredith couldn't stop smiling as she looked around the yacht. Its spacious deck shone in the soft light of the ship's lanterns. Jeff walked over to one of the crew members, and gave him brief instructions. Immediately he returned and wrapped his arms around her. Within a short time the boat was on its way, edging quietly out of the harbor.

"Oh, Jeff, this is marvelous! How in the world did you manage it all?"

"It's a loan from a good friend, an old fraternity brother of mine."

"Thank him for me. I have a feeling I'll never forget this night."

"That's what it's all about, Meri."

As they glided out of the harbor, they watched the sailboats playing along the bay. Sails gleamed golden as the last remnants of a fading sun caught them in its grasp. Meri reached for Jeff's arm, squeezing it a little tighter. Jeff responded by bringing her a little closer to him.

The pop from a cork startled her and she glanced around abruptly. The waiter smiled, then began to pour champagne into two crystal glasses. To Meredith's delight he placed them on a small silver tray, which he brought over to them. Tonight she felt like a fairy princess being charmed by her prince.

"Dinner will be ready in ten minutes, sir," the waiter told Jeff.

Meredith waited until he was out of hearing distance, then giggled nervously. "Jeff, what are you up to?"

"Is my lady pleased?"

"You know I am!"

"Then, let's offer a toast, shall we?"

"All right. What shall we drink to?"

"To the most beautiful woman in the world, my very special lady."

As they sipped from their glasses, Meredith looked deep into Jeff's eyes. She nestled against him, mesmerized by the moonlight dancing on the waves. Before long, dinner was set on the table. Jeff pulled a chair for her, then walked around and seated himself opposite her.

Immediately, the waiter brought their entrée, shrimp cocktail with a delicious piquant sauce. Meredith ate alowly, savoring the delicate flavors. The meal progressed leisurely as they dined on several courses. Finally, as the dessert was placed before them, an exquisite *mousse au chocolat*, Meredith found herself totally relaxed and utterly delighted. When the last morsels had disappeared, the waiter emerged with a bottle of Courvoisier. He poured the special brandy into small glasses, and, again, served them from a silver tray.

Meredith's eyes rested on Jeff as they savored the strong liquid. She saw his eyes linger on her throat, then drop to her breasts. His vision alone served to caress her. She felt the blood rushing through her veins and the rapid hammering of her heart as her body yearned for his.

"Meredith, I have something for you."

Jeff reached into his coat pocket, and handed her a small velvet-covered box. Meredith's hands trembled in anticipation as she accepted it. She sat staring at it for a few moments, then opened it. There in the center, nestled in the smooth lining, was an exquisite diamond ring. One huge emerald-cut stone had been mounted on a yellow-gold band. It was breathtaking in its simplicity.

Speechless, Meredith continued to stare. Through a fog, she heard Jeff talking to her.

"It was my grandmother's engagement ring. I wanted you to have it. Try it on and see how it fits."

Carefully she extracted the ring from its case, then trembling with excitement allowed Jeff to slip it on her finger. The ring settled on her hand perfectly. Meredith saw the diamond shimmer and dance under the lights of the boat, causing small rainbows to appear on the surface of the deck.

"Jeff, this is the most perfect day of my entire life. Do you realize how happy you've made me?"

"I'll always try to make you happy, Meri. I'll never give you cause to regret today."

As their evening drew to a close, the boat silently edged back to the pier. Small lights from other boats flickered in the darkness, while in the distance the lights of the city sparkled, reminding Meredith of a brightly colored Christmas tree.

When they docked, Jeff took her hand and kissed it lightly. "Meri, I love you more than anything in this world."

Gently touching the side of his face, she answered softly. "I love you too, Jeff. I'll try to be a good wife."

Hand in hand they left the boat and walked down the pier, toward the car. Jeff helped her inside, then eased himself behind the wheel.

"Shall we go to my place?" he suggested. "You've never seen it."

"That sounds interesting. I'm curious to see what

your bachelor's lair looks like."

Jeff chuckled. "Well, you know the saying. 'Come to my parlor, said the spider to the fly.'"

After a twenty-minute drive they arrived at a secluded residential area. Meredith, expecting an apartment, was surprised at the size of his home. The lighting in front illuminated areas of the front yard, and she was amazed to see how well kept it seemed.

"Are you an amateur gardener?"

"No," he replied candidly, "but I do like to get my hands in the soil when there's time."

Once inside, Meredith glanced around, taking in every detail. It was a beautiful home. Although not pretentious, it was by no means modest. The sprawling interior was decorated in dark tones, matching the wood paneling that seemed present everywhere she looked. A huge fireplace occupied the far wall. On the side walls, tall oak bookshelves were filled to capacity with volumes of books. A massive leather-bound sofa was placed directly across the fireplace, with two comfortable oversized chairs on each side. The dark pine coffee table in front of the sofa looked as if it belonged in the captain's cabin of an old sailing vessel.

From the entryway, she could see parts of the kitchen, on her right. Not wishing to appear rude, Meredith waited for an invitation before continuing to explore.

"Go on!" he urged. "Look to your heart's content. *Mi casa es tu casa,* like the Spanish say."

Meredith grinned shyly, then wandered down the corridor. The first room she saw was a small study. Here again the wood paneling added an extra sense of warmth. A rather large antique secretary took up much of the space. A small bathroom was next, and she was quick to notice that it had recently been redone. The fixtures were brand new and finished in a lovely pale blue. The last room on the right had been converted into a game room. Most of the area was dominated by a massive pool table. Cues were neatly stacked on a wall rack, and a small wet bar with tall wooden stools faced into the room from one wall.

On the opposite side of the hall was the master bedroom. It was finished in the best of taste. The furniture was all obviously antique. A large oak four-poster bed was the focal point. Two hand-carved nightstands flanked the bed, and one wall was filled from side to side with two enormous armoires.

The last room was much smaller and, she surmised, used as a guest room. Meredith, impressed by his taste, walked slowly back to the living room. Jeff had lit a fire and motioned for her to sit next to him.

Meredith settled beside him and accepted a glass of brandy. Leaning against him, she sighed and stared at the fire.

After a few minutes, she spoke. "Jeff, your taste is impeccable. This home is lovely."

"I'm glad you think so. It makes it easier for me to ask you something I've been thinking about."

Meredith looked up, eyebrows furrowed.

Jeff continued slowly. "I've done a lot of work on this place and I've grown to like it immensely. How would you feel if we made it our home? You could change whatever you wanted, and there's plenty of room for your furniture."

"Jeff, I love this place! If this is where you want to stay, that's fine. I can't think of anything I'd change. As for as my furniture, well, besides an old cedar chest I picked up at a garage sale, I haven't got any."

"Your place is furnished?"

Meredith nodded.

"If you want frilly curtains or anything like that, let me know. I can put them up for you."

Meredith laughed, then cocked her head to one side. "Do I really look like the type?"

"No, I guess you don't. Not to worry. Your moose head is more than welcome over the fireplace."

"No thanks. If I want anybody's head stuck through a wall, it'll be yours."

"Now we're getting brave. I should be a gentleman, of course, and warn you that it's positively suicidal to try and get tough with me."

"You know what?" Meredith smiled coyly. "You're highly overrated."

Jeff shook his head in mock disapproval. "Don't start what you can't finish."

"My, my, we're testy today!" Pausing, she added, "Are your Fruit of the Looms too tight, dear?"

"Again, as a gentleman, I warn you," Jeff said with an exaggerated leer. "People who give me a hard time have a habit of disappearing."

"I knew it! You're just another pretty face who's stuck for an answer after someone says hello."

Jeff stood up slowly.

"Resorting to violence again!" Meredith shook her head sadly.

"All right. One last chance. If you start apologizing profusely, I might consider forgiving you."

"Oh my! What next! The rape-and-pillage scene?"

Jeff grinned, his eyes sparkling with deviltry. "Wishful thinking?"

Meredith glanced around her. "I don't have to worry. Your instruction manual isn't here, and I know you'd be lost without it!"

Jeff grabbed her hand and pulled her toward him. Ruffling her hair, he held both her hands inside one massive one, in a tight grip.

"Hey, not fair! Let go of my hands, you big bully, so I can fight back."

Jeff laughed and pulled her against him. His mouth took hers savagely, leaving her breathless. Meredith pushed closer, feeling the fire of his touch. His lips caressed the base of her throat while he gently eased down the zipper of her dress.

His mouth possessed hers once more, demanding her surrender. Weakness spread through her, leaving her receptive and eager for the pleasures he would bring. Undressing her with slow, sure movements, he watched her garments fall to the floor, one by one. Meredith, eager to find the right ways to please him, rose to her feet and offered her hand in a silent gesture.

Jeff moved closer to her. His eyes held a mixture of hunger and admiration. Caressing the soft curves of her body, he waited as she slowly undressed him, encouraging her to share in his pleasure. When her hands, warm and soft, touched him, he moaned and tried to press her against him.

Meredith pushed away gently. Trembling, she slipped off his last piece of clothing. When she had finished, she stared at him with unabashed wonder. His muscles rippled and tightened as she touched him with exquisite gentleness. Jeff's strong hands pressed against the sides of her waist, then moved up and down, slowly stroking her silky flesh. Her eyes were wide as they locked with his. Her parted lips were quivering.

Melding her soft contours against his own hard and masculine body, he covered her mouth with kisses and ran his tongue over her lips. He kissed her again, deeply, and then, in one swift movement, he lifted her into his arms and carried her to his bed. His eyes roamed over her still figure. When she moved toward him, straining for closer contact, he encircled her waist, pulling her harshly against him.

Nothing else mattered now, save the fact they belonged together. Seeking the warming comfort of a lover's touch, they sealed their future in a breathless encounter. Love's radiant promise was made whole, enriched by their lifetime commitment to each other.

Snuggled against his chest, Meredith felt content and secure. Hearing the grandfather clock chime the hour, she sat up and brushed her hair from her face. "It's time for me to get back to the hotel."

"You could stay here. . . ."

"I don't have any of my things here. It'll be easier if you take me back tonight."

Jeff sat up reluctantly. "All right, if that's what you want."

"Trust me. It'll be easier. I like lots of time to get ready in the morning. If you take me back tomorrow, then we'll have to get up at least two hours earlier. It's pretty late now. I think you'll appreciate it more in the morning."

Jeff chuckled. "You're probably right."

Grabbing his clothes, he dressed quickly, then walked to the living room. Meredith emerged a few minutes later. Escorting her to his car, he drove her back to the hotel.

As he started to get out of the car, Meredith placed her hand on his arm. "No, don't worry about seeing me to my room."

"I'm not worried about it, but I'm still taking you upstairs."

Accompanying her through the lobby, he led her into the elevator, then to her door. "Would you consider getting married right away? We can always postpone the honeymoon until later."

"Oh, Jeff, it won't be much longer. It would really

be better for both of us if we waited until we could take a few weeks off."

"All right." His eyes gleamed. "See how easy I am to get along with? It's a wonderful trait for a husband to have. I hope you appreciate it."

"Oh, I do! I'm grateful for every little bit." She gave him a playful wink.

Jeff leaned over and kissed her lightly. "Good night, sweetheart."

As he headed for the elevator, Meredith closed her eyes and sighed, filled with blissful sweetness.

The next morning, Meredith arrived at the base earlier than she had planned. Deciding to start work immediately, she began filling out reports and compiling data to be fed into the computer. The malfunction had to be found—and quickly. Time, under the new guidelines issued by her superiors, was becoming critical. Meredith worked most of the morning uninterrupted. After a quick sandwich at her desk, she returned to the Scorpio, paperwork in hand.

She began reviewing specifications with some of the factory personnel, when a series of wolf whistles sounded inside the hanger. Meredith glanced around. Walking toward the offices was the most stunning woman she had ever seen! Tall, with shoulder-length blonde hair, the woman moved with the sleek grace of a tiger. When she turned, their eyes locked for a brief second. Meredith knew she had been evaluated by the deep emerald eyes. Wondering who this woman was, Meredith resolved to go back to her office as soon as possible. She told the men what she wanted done, then turned and walked back upstairs. As she arrived at the second floor, Meredith glimpsed the young woman running toward someone. It was Jeff! In a split second she was in his arms, kissing him passionately.

Tears filled her eyes until she could no longer see. Was this the same man who promised his love to her the night before? How could she have been so trusting? Suddenly feeling cheap and used, Meredith closed the door to her office and locked it. She sat down and allowed silent tears to drop unhindered from her eyes.

After a few minutes there was a knock on her door. Meredith, with an effort, tried to keep her voice steady. "One moment, please."

Wiping the tears away, she pulled the compact from her purse and hid the telltale signs. "Come in."

There, framing her door, was Jeff. "Bill said you were in the hall when Nicole arrived."

Nicole? Meredith wondered silently. Somehow the name suited the exotic beauty she had seen. In comparison she felt ugly and inadequate.

"Honey, Nicole and I go back a long ways. She's no threat to you. She's left now, so why don't you come to my office so we can talk."

Meredith swallowed hard, trying to keep her voice even and detached. "Not here, Jeff."

"All right. Dinner tonight. Say six-thirty?"

"Yes."

Meredith shut everything from her mind. Mechanically going through the motions for the rest of the day, she was relieved when it was finally time to go home.

Deliberately trying to avoid the others, Meredith waited in her office an extra fifteen minutes, then left for the parking lot. As she crossed the concrete area in front of the hangar, she spotted the same beautiful woman she had seen earlier, walking toward her.

"Oh, no!" Meredith murmured softly to herself.

She waited, trying to appear confident and composed, for her to approach. When they finally met face to face, Meredith was once again aware of the sharp contrast between them.

"So you finally came out! I've been waiting for ages in my car. Jeff told me about you. It seems you are my competition."

Fighting a sick feeling in the pit of her stomach, Meredith replied icily. "I don't know what you mean."

"You mean Jeff never told you about me?"

"No."

With a smug, satisfied smile, she continued. "My dear, Jeff and I were engaged. Actually, we never really broke up. I went away for awhile, but as you can see I've returned. I intend to get him back. He still loves me, you know."

"You're out of your mind."

"No, he's mine and always will be. I don't want to argue, I just wanted to warn you. Prepare yourself. You won't have him much longer."

"We'll have to see about that!"

"Well, if you insist on competing with me, that's your business. You'll soon realize the futility of that gesture. I don't want to hurt you; after all, you're only a stranger. I just wanted to warn you I've come to reclaim what's mine."

Flashing the same confident smile, she whirled around and quickly walked away.

Meredith fought to keep her hands steady. She wouldn't give Nicole the satisfaction of knowing she had achieved just what she had set out to do. She now desperately feared she would lose the man she loved and wanted more than anything in the world.

Driving back to the hotel, Meredith could hardly keep her foot from flooring the accelerator pedal. Somehow pushing the little car to its limits seemed to assuage some of her anger. The car was one of the few things she could control at the moment.

Resolving not to look inconsequential compared to Nicole, Meredith spent twice the length of time she normally did dressing. Wearing a deep burgandy evening dress and shoes to match, she stood back, judging her reflection in the mirror. Whirling around, Meredith threw her brush savagely on the bed. Why couldn't she radiate the same extra something Nicole seemed to possess? The easy grace, that subtle charm.

She glanced at the clock and sighed. Jeff would arrive soon. Swallowing convulsively, she tried to ease the dryness at the back of her throat. Instinct warned her there was danger ahead. Nicole had made it clear she wanted Jeff back. Meredith bit her lower lip. Would she be any kind of match for a woman like Nicole?

A knock at the door interrupted her thoughts. Meredith took a deep breath, then walked to the door and opened it.

"Hi! Are you ready?" Jeff asked.

"Sure!"

Jeff took the keys from her hand and locked the door. In a familiar gesture, he wrapped his arm around her waist as they continued toward the elevator. Silently they rode down and made their way to the car.

"You're awfully quiet."

"I don't feel like saying much right now," Meredith replied.

"I had no idea you were this upset. Don't you trust me?"

"Of course I do! Am I acting that badly?"

"You tell me."

"Jeff, I'm sorry. I don't mean to."

"Meri, all you need to know is that I love you and only you. What Nicole and I had is over and done with."

Meredith nodded silently. She was acting like a jealous witch. Resolving to make it up to him, she smiled. Reaching for his hand, she pressed it to her lips. "I love you, Jeff. I don't want you to be angry with me."

Meredith saw his eyes soften. "I'm not angry. I'll tell you what. It's a bit early for dinner. How about a walk on the beach?"

"That sounds lovely," she murmured.

Jeff drove for a while, then pulled off to the side of the road. Meredith could hear the sound of the waves crashing upon the shore. The sun was about to set and hung just above the water. Jeff helped her out of the car and led the way to the beach. Walking hand in hand, they reveled in the spell of the moment.

Stopping by a tall pine, Jeff drew her toward him. Hidden in the shadows, his lips searched for hers, possessing them in a fiery kiss that sent chills down her spine. Feeling her tremble in expectation, Jeff continued to caress her as his mouth slipped down her neck and to her throat. A low moan escaped Meredith's lips. Pressing against him, she closed her eyes in a gesture of surrender. Tenderly, he sought her lips once more, then, forcing her mouth open, slid his tongue inside, tasting, exploring. Meredith could hear his breathing become labored, and her own matching his. Their kiss seemed to last an eternity.

His hands slid down and cupped her breasts tightly. Meredith felt her knees turn to water as he erotically kneaded her pliant flesh. His searing breath exploded against her neck.

The rippling emotions coursing through her forced her to press nearer to him. Seeking the comfort of his kiss, she pressed her mouth against his. As she caught his tongue between her lips, she sucked gently. In a frenzy of desire, Jeff tore his mouth away from hers, slowly dropping to her breasts. The warmth of his breath worked through her garments, causing her flesh to tingle. Meredith shuddered as Jeff's hands moved slowly down her body. Clinging desperately to him, she felt his hardness pressing against her. Her hand drifted downward, seeking to please him. Jeff inhaled sharply; a muffled animal sound came from his throat. Slowly, Meredith pulled away.

Jeff stood for a moment, passion burning in his eyes. "Yes, I think you're right. I'm too tempted to take you right here and now."

Meredith, trembling, moved a little further away. Jeff, immediately aware, laughed. "Don't worry, kitten. I have no intention of making love to you here." He waved a complacent hand at the open beach area around them.

Meredith laughed and placed her hand securely inside his as they walked to the car. How she loved him! He belonged to her as much as she belonged to him. Nicole would not get him away from her so easily.

Jeff drove slowly to the restaurant. Although he kept one hand firmly on the wheel, his other grasped Meredith's hand. "Do you realize what you do to me?"

"Do you realize what it does to me when you touch me or kiss me?"

He smiled. "A lot, I hope."

Jeff parked near the entrance of his favorite restaurant. With his arm encircled tightly about her waist, they went inside. The maître d' escorted them to a table overlooking the bay. Meredith sighed contentedly as he ordered her favorite brand of sherry, without needing to ask.

The waiter brought the drinks, and Meredith casually sipped the sweet liquid. She was aware of the way Jeff's eyes nestled on her. With a shy grin, he looked out the window toward the ships in the bay. Seconds later, as if warned by a sixth sense, Meredith turned her attention back to Jeff. His face had turned cold and hard. Surprised, she followed his gaze. There, at a table across the room, sat Mike and Nicole. The fear and insecurity she had felt earlier came rushing back. What hold did that woman have on him? Was it jealousy she saw in his face? To her horror, Nicole stood and walked over to their table.

"Well, hello. Let us buy you another round and we'll have dinner together."

Not giving Meredith a chance to reply, Nicole motioned for Mike to come over. Soon they were seated with them. Meredith felt hopelessly inadequate as Nicole charmed both men. Her easy banter seemed to enchant them as they focused all their attention on her. Meredith, feeling neglected and ignored, ate little.

When everyone had finished eating, Nicole took Jeff's hand. Meredith fought the anger that enveloped her as Jeff complied to her request for a dance. Jeff seemed to have forgotten all about her. Minutes ago, when he had professed his love, she had believed and hung on every word. Now, seeing Nicole and him together made her realize Nicole still had a hold on him. She had been a momentary distraction, nothing more. His love was totally and completely within Nicole's reach.

"Let's dance," she heard Mike say as he led her to the dance floor.

Meredith, in a daze, followed. In Mike's arms she went through the motions of dancing, trying to fight the terrible numbness that spread through her.

"He isn't worth it, Meredith."

"What?" she asked, still in a state of bewilderment.

"Meredith, I told you once before. Jeff isn't the type of man a woman can hold on to for long."

"Nicole seems to have him entranced. . . ."

"Nicole is every man's dream. She can arouse feelings most of us never even realized we could have.

With Jeff she had an advantage. He loved her once, and Meredith, I hate to tell you this, but he's still in love with her."

"No!" Meredith protested, choking back tears.

"Honey, just look at them!"

Meredith looked around the dance floor, unable to locate either one of them. "Mike, where did they go?"

Mike glanced around and, unable to find them, shrugged. "Does it really matter?"

"Yes, it matters!" she almost screamed.

Sensing her panic, Mike spoke softly. "All right, Meri. I'll help you look, but you may not like what you find."

"I've got to find them," Meredith replied dully.

"They may have gone for a walk on the pier. Let's go out to the balcony. We'll be able to see farther from there."

When they neared the balcony, Meredith could see two shadows under the moonlight. As the light from a passing boat illuminated the scene below, she gasped. There was Jeff cradling Nicole in his arms. Lost in the passion of the moment, his body was locked against hers.

Meredith's heart constricted. Turning abruptly, she ran out of the restaurant to escape the harsh reality. Fighting the sick feeling of loneliness, she tried to clear her thoughts.

Mike, catching up to her, grasped her shoulders firmly. "Don't run away from me like that! You scared the daylights out of me. I didn't know what you were going to do!"

Meredith looked at him, tears welling in her eyes. Empathizing with the hurt and pain visible in her eyes, Mike relented and took her hand. "Come with me. You need to get away from here. Let's walk down the pier for a bit."

Meredith tried to regain some semblance of control. The anguish of knowing that Jeff's promises had been worthless ripped her apart. The one thing she had valued most in her life had been torn from her and there seemed no way of getting it back.

"Oh, Mike!" Meredith sobbed.

Mike held her tightly against him. "Meri, he's a bum. He's always been that way. He's only concerned with himself. He's just not worth it."

# - 8 -

MIKE WAS HOLDING her tight within the circle of his arms. From the corner of her eye Meredith saw Jeff march toward them. He stopped less than a foot away and glared at Mike. His features twisted into something very ugly. "Meredith, I want to talk to you."

Meredith pulled away from Mike, swallowed, and looked directly at Jeff. "We don't have anything to discuss."

"Come on. I'll take you back. We can talk it out in the car."

"Sorry. Mike's taking me home."

"Meredith, don't be so damn stubborn. I can explain. . . ."

"I'm not interested in any explanation, Jeff. Like I told you, Mike will take me back to the hotel. You can go back and kiss Nicole all you like without worrying about me."

Muttering an oath under his breath, Jeff took a

quick step toward her. Mike instantly took a step forward, intercepting him. "Back off. She's with me now."

"Don't push it, mister. Get out of the way."

"As you can see, the lady isn't interested in what you have to say."

Jeff's eyes were snapping and his fists were clenched tightly. Mike, not giving an inch, continued to block his advance.

Jeff kept his voice even. "Meredith, unless you want me to flatten him, I suggest you tell him to get lost."

Mike looked at Jeff steadily. "Take another step and you'll kiss the sand."

"Jeff," Meredith said softly. "You've done enough tonight. Go!"

Jeff's eyes narrowed with a new surge of anger. "Trust," he said. "All right, Meri. If that's the way you want it."

It wasn't what she wanted at all! Why had Nicole come back? Everything was in such a jumble. She wanted to go back to her room and be left alone.

As quickly as it had erupted, the confrontation ended. Jeff turned casually as if the matter no longer merited his attention.

Meredith choked back a tear as she watched him leave. Aware of Mike close at her side, she struggled to compose herself. "I'd like to go back now. Would you mind?"

"Not at all."

Driving slowly, Mike tried to distract her thoughts. Placing his hand over hers, he gave it a gentle squeeze. "It's okay, Meri. You're not all alone in this. I'll be there if you need me."

"Thanks," she whispered.

Feeling nothing except a curious void, Meredith glanced at the passing cars. When they arrived, she didn't wait for Mike. Gathering her things, she left the car.

"Wait, Meri. I'll walk you upstairs."

Meredith waited, saying nothing. When they arrived at her door, she wished him a good night.

"Meri, I can't leave you like this. Let me come inside for a few minutes."

"I'll be all right."

"Please."

Relenting, Meredith stepped aside and allowed him in. Sitting on the edge of the bed, she stared numbly at her hands. Mike came over and sat beside her. When she began to cry, he pressed her against him, brushing her hair tenderly.

Meredith jumped when the telephone rang, echoing loudly in the silent room. Watching it for several rings, she hesitated to pick up the receiver.

"Want me to get that?" Mike asked.

"No. It's all right. I'll get it. It might be important."

Meredith heard Jeff's voice plainly over the wire. "Meredith, I've got to talk to you. Don't hang up, please!"

"Jeff, just leave me alone!"

Mike took the receiver from her hand. "Let me handle this." Seeing her reluctance, he added, "Please."

Meredith relinquished the telephone and sat on one of the chairs.

"Jeff, this is Mike. Look, you've given the lady a bad enough time tonight. You've had your fun. Now lay off."

Mike placed the receiver back in its cradle, then glanced at Meredith. "Want to take the telephone off the hook?"

Meredith nodded. "You're a good friend, Mike. Thanks for everything."

Mike stood and kissed her lightly on the forehead.

"I'll always be your friend, Meri. Call on me anytime, if you need me."

Meredith smiled and thanked him. When he left, tears came freely as she no longer attempted to control the bitterness she felt. Tomorrow she would return his ring. Sobbing into her pillows, Meredith fell into a fitful sleep.

The next morning she arrived at work early. Not trusting herself to face Jeff, she slipped the ring from her finger and placed it inside the top drawer of his desk. Without looking back, she returned to her office and began to work. The rest of the morning evolved with the usual problems, but Meredith was spared seeing Jeff. At lunch Mike came by holding two enormous sandwiches.

"I come bearing gifts, gorgeous."

Smiling, Meredith helped him inside. "You're so sweet!"

"That's what friends are for, I'm told."

Meredith kissed him lightly on the cheek. "Someday, maybe, I'll be able to pay you back."

"Don't worry. I'm not keeping score, you know."

Hearing footsteps, Meredith glanced at the hall. Jeff stopped at the doorway. A look of unmasked hatred passed between the two men. Jeff didn't even look at her before he wheeled away and walked rapidly down the corridor. Meredith exhaled loudly.

"It'll hurt for a long time, sugar, but I'll help any way I can," Mike said.

"I don't fool you for one second, do I?"

"We don't have to keep secrets from one another."

Meredith looked up as Mike's hand gently covered hers. "It's okay, Meri. It won't always hurt like this. Besides, you have me and I'm pretty good company."

Meredith smiled sadly. "You are very good company and, in case you don't already know it, I don't have the foggiest idea what I'd do without you."

"Good. I like to know I'm indispensable."

Picking up the remains of their lunch, they returned the office to normal. As they drifted back to work, Meredith attempted to shut out the pain and all the distraction around her, trying to concentrate solely on the aircraft. It seemed to her only moments had passed, when Mike peered inside.

"Hey, sexy, how about dinner with me tonight? Something simple, say pizza, at my place?"

Meredith automatically glanced at the clock. Her face registered surprise. "It is quitting time already?"

"Sure is. How about it?"

"I'll tell you what. Let me offer a counterproposal. How about I treat you to dinner and I pick the place."

"Spurning my pizza?"

"No, I'd like a rain check on that, but I have a better idea."

"Sounds intriguing. What time should I pick you up?"

"About an hour and a half from now, and wear jeans."

"You got it. Do I get a hint?"

"Do you like hot dogs?"

"Sure." Mike waited a second. "Is that my hint?"

"That's it."

"Okay, then. I'll see you later."

Meredith carefully placed the classified papers in the safe, then straightened out her desk. She strode out of the building quickly, not wanting anything to delay her plans for the evening. Driving out of base, she headed for the grocery store. After buying hot dogs, buns, chips, and a few other treats, she returned to the hotel. Selecting a pair of blue jeans and a faded blue sweater, she braided her hair into pigtails that fastened at the base of her neck, then wrapped a light blue velvet ribbon over each.

When she finished stacking all the food inside the woven basket she had purchased for the occasion, Meredith realized she had bought nothing to drink. A knock sounded. After a quick glance into the mirror, she walked to the door and opened it.

Mike looked at her and chuckled. "You look adorable. Like a little girl!"

"Thanks . . . I think."

"Well, sweet stuff, where are we going?"

Meredith pointed to the basket. "I thought we'd build a campfire on the beach and roast hot dogs."

Mike laughed. "You're kidding."

"No, why? Don't you like the idea?

"With you for company, anything's perfect. I just haven't done that kind of thing for years."

"Neither have I. That's why I thought it would be fun. There's only one problem. I forgot to get something to drink."

"No problem. Shall we get some wine?"

"What goes with hot dogs, red or white?" Meredith laughed.

"Neither. How about Cokes?"

"That sounds better."

"You have a beach picked out?"

"No, that's your department. You didn't think I'd do all the work?"

Mike, smiling, tugged at one of her pigtails. "Let's go. I think I know the perfect place."

"Pick someplace where there are sticks."

"Sticks?"

"Yes, as in the kind you need for a campfire."

"Real outdoorsy, aren't you kid!"

"Don't tell me it shows!"

"A bit."

Mike helped Meredith load the supplies into his car. Before she had a chance to get in, he went to her side and held the door open for her. Thanking him, she wondered about the change in his manners.

After a short drive, Mike stopped and picked up a cold six-pack and some Cokes. Bringing them back to the car, he placed them on the floor in the rear.

"Hope you don't mind. I thought I'd bring some beer along."

"Ugh."

"I take it you don't like beer."

"I think it tastes terrible," Meredith said, wrinkling her nose.

"Well, don't drink any. Do you mind if I have some?"

"No, of course not."

Mike continued driving, while Meredith, content to just sit back, relaxed. With Mike she never felt pressured. She could be herself and be completely at ease. The rush of emotions and the fiery passion Jeff evoked in her was absent, but that made for a much more relaxed atmosphere. Thinking of Jeff, Meredith felt a cold numbness creep through her. Mike must have sensed her sudden change of mood, because he took her hand. His grip was firm yet gentle. Meredith remembered the firmness of Jeff's touch almost instantly, then shook her head.

"Forget him, Meri. It won't do any good to keep going over the past. That much I have learned. Let it go."

Nodding silently, Meredith focused her attention on the passing scenery. Mike patted her hand, then returned his to the steering wheel. After a very long drive, he stopped the car and parked. Meredith could see the beach directly ahead, through a grove of tall pines.

"This is it. The drive's kinda long, but it's a beautiful beach."

Meredith helped Mike carry food as they walked

onto the sandy area. Picking a spot, she carefully placed their things down. In no time, Mike managed to find enough wood to start a very small fire.

Their impromptu picnic was a success. The two, enjoying each other's company, talked about anything that came to mind. When they were finished eating, Meredith placed what was left back into the basket and relaxed, sipping a Coke.

"Let's go for a little walk," Mike suggested.

"Leave all the things here?"

"Sure. We won't go far."

"All right."

Mike helped Meredith up, and they began to stroll close to the water's edge. While they made small talk, Mike casually placed his arm around her shoulders. The air was crisp for autumn, but it wasn't cold. The murmur of the sea soothed her as they ambled along at a leisurely pace. The moon and the stars barely illuminated their path, yet she felt comfortable in the darkness. As they reversed their course and headed back to the campfire, Meredith sighed. She felt strangely at peace here. The hurt still lingered, but sharing the pain had made it more bearable. She was grateful for her new friend.

Sitting by the fire, Mike reclined on his side and toyed with the sand in front of him. In an attempt to satisfy his curiosity, he began to ask questions about her life. Normally she would have refused to answer them, but tonight it was easy to confide.

"Meri, have you ever wondered what your life would have been like had you not gone to college but had married instead?"

"Most of my friends did just that. For a long time I really felt like an oddball. Then, again, I wanted my career so badly I never could see myself doing anything else."

"If things had worked out between Carey and me, I'd have had a couple of kids by now."

"She hurt you very badly, didn't she?"

"Yes," he replied almost inaudibly.

When Meredith reached to touch him, Mike's eyes softened and he smiled. "You're sweet, but you don't have to worry about me. I'm over that now."

"I wonder if I'll ever be."

"You will, honey."

Meredith laid back on the sand and stared at the star-filled sky above her. "I really can't blame Jeff. Nicole is absolutely ravishing."

Mike moved closer to her, resting on one elbow. "You're just as beautiful, Meri."

"Sure I am."

"You are," he murmured, then leaned over to kiss her. Meredith turned her head sharply, but Mike's hand steadied her. "Meri, I'm not going to ask anything from you, but I know I can make you forget Jeff. Even if only for a little while. We're only friends. There's no danger between us."

"There's also no love."

"Yes, there's love. Perhaps not the same as you feel for Jeff, but it's there. You're denying it to yourself as well as to me."

Mike leaned over her, his eyes soft and loving. Slowly his lips met hers and he pressed gently against them. Pulling away from her long enough to look down at her face, he came down against her once more. Sensing her detachment, he stood and brushed the sand from his jeans. "I guess it's too soon. I shouldn't have pressed it."

"Mike, I really do like you. I'm sorry if I've been a disappointment."

"I'll live."

Meredith, aware her response had hurt him, looked at him thoughtfully. What was she doing? Jeff was

out of her life for good. It was time she faced that
fact. Mike had shown her only kindness and this had
been the way she had repaid him. "Mike?" Reaching
for his hand, she pulled him down onto the sand.
"Kiss me again, but this time give me a chance, all
right?"

When he hesitated, she pulled him toward her. Her
lips sought his, timidly at first but gaining confidence
with each passing second. Parting her lips slightly,
she invited his advance. After a few minutes, she
pushed him back gently. "Now that wasn't so bad,
was it?"

Mike smiled. "No, it sure wasn't."

Meredith looked away, feeling a twinge of sadness.
Purposefully avoiding his eyes, she tried to banish
Jeff from her mind. It had been pleasant to kiss Mike,
but nothing more. She wanted Jeff and needed him
more than ever. Perhaps she had given up too easily.
Intrigued by the thought, her eyebrows furrowed. Yes,
perhaps if she fought for him . . .

"Meri, you won't always love him, you know. I
realize at the moment I'm only a substitute, but I have
time."

Meredith, alerted, turned her attention to him.
"What?"

"Meri, I think it's time I told you the truth. Perhaps
then you'll be able to understand me more. I fell in
love with you the moment I saw you. I've wanted to
warn you about Jeff, but there was no way I could
have done more than I did. When he hurt you I wanted
to tear him apart. All I want is for you to let me love
you. Someday, maybe, you'll learn to love me too."

The declaration stunned her. How blind she had
been! If she had only known, she could have kept
from hurting him. She knew the sting of rejection and
had no wish to inflict it on anyone. Especially someone who had been as kind as he. Feeling an immense

empathy for him, she reached for and touched the side of his face, and caressed it gently.

"Mike, I never knew. I'm the last person you should have trusted with your love. There's only one man for me. If I can't have him, then I guess I'll have to end up with nothing. If I turned to you, I'd only be using you, and in the end I'd hurt you more."

"Will you at least give us a chance?"

"Mike, it's no use. He's all I think about."

"All right. If I can't have you any other way, then I can at least be a friend you can turn to whenever you need one."

"Mike, listen to me. I'd only be using you. Don't you see that?"

"Perhaps that's the way it would begin, but someday you may learn to love me. I'm willing to chance it."

"I'll end up hurting you, and I don't want to do that. I honestly don't."

"Fair enough," he conceded after a long pause, "but don't make me stop seeing you."

Picking up the basket and the Coke bottles, Meredith merely shook her head. Things would never be the same between them. Feeling the added sorrow of losing a friend, she longed for the quiet and solace of her room. She needed to sort things out. Mike drove her back, with scarcely a word exchanged between them. When they arrived at the hotel, he escorted her to her room.

"Good night, Meri. Please don't worry. I want us to remain friends. I will never pressure you or ask anything of you until you offer it willingly."

"I want you to understand how things stand. I don't want to mislead you."

"I know that. Don't worry. Really. We are good friends and we do have a lot of fun together, don't we?"

"Sure!"

"All right then."

Smiling, Mike kissed her on the forehead. He turned and walked toward the elevator. Meredith closed the door, then stretched out on the bed. Poor Mike! This had been her fault. She should have seen it coming.

# - 9 -

BY THE TIME Meredith arrived at work, the team of factory specialists at the site had still not managed to locate the source of the problem. The current theory was that it had been a fluke that had corrected itself. Meredith argued bitterly, reasoning that they could not have possibly corrected a problem that had never been identified. After hours of heated discussions a compromise was reached.

A brand-new aircraft was scheduled to be delivered in a few days. The prototype now on base would be returned, and the new arrival would be used for the trials, along with the trouble-free trainer. It was then that Meredith was forced to accept what would undoubtedly become the least savory part of the testing. Thinking of the gentle roll and sway of the giant carriers, Meredith felt herself turning green.

Given the task of informing the test pilots of their decision, Meredith felt her hands turn cold. She had hoped for a moment with Jeff, but not one where they would meet as adversaries. There was no escaping it now. Somehow she had to make Jeff understand and accept a fact that would undoubtedly infuriate him.

Meredith tried to think of a way but could find none. It was simply part of her job. To delegate it would be the same as admitting she no longer was able to function as project manager. Stopping to get a drink at the water fountain, Meredith was aware of the uneasy feeling in the pit of her stomach. Regardless of the way she felt, she had to keep Jeff from seeing or sensing her nervousness. She would have to be firm and professional in her approach.

Meredith climbed the stairs slowly. Walking to Jeff's office, she knocked on the door.

"Come in."

Meredith entered. Standing in front of his desk, she gave him a chance to complete the form he was filling out. When he finally looked up, Meredith swallowed hard. Their eyes met for an instant. Glancing away, she took a deep breath. In the most businesslike tone she could muster, she spoke.

"I've been told the malfunction in the Scorpio was not caused by a design deficiency. In case the difficulty was caused by a faulty subsystem, we are going to have a brand-new prototype delivered in a couple of days. Be ready for a five-day test cruise."

Jeff's eyes rested on her. The softness of his gaze quickly gave way to a cold rage. "What you're really saying is that no one has been able to pinpoint what went wrong, and your darling computer isn't much help, so you've all decided to have another prototype delivered to see if that solves the problem for you."

"All the systems have been checked by our people and yours. We believe it was probably a part incorrectly manufactured. A minor factory error. We are sending the aircraft back for reassembly."

"Meanwhile, I'm supposed to fly the other one and see what happens. Just like that," he said, snapping his fingers.

"That's your job, yes."

"You really don't give a . . ." Stopping abruptly, he looked away from her. "Yes, it's my job. If that's all you came by to say, I've got work to do."

Meredith turned and left his office. Any chance of a reconciliation had just gone out the window. Fighting the bitterness she felt, she strode angrily down the hall. They seemed destined to remain in opposite corners. Why was it they couldn't talk it out and patch things up as other people could? Disgusted, she picked up a cup of coffee from the machine. What she really wanted was a drink, but this would have to do during business hours. It would all have been so simple if she had fallen in love with Mike. He was always considerate and eager to please her.

As the day dragged on, Meredith continued her work automatically, going through the motions. Her thoughts kept returning to Jeff and Nicole. She had to get him back, but on her own terms. She would never again share him with another woman.

When the work day came to an end, the staff began to leave. Meredith had not seen Mike all day. Wondering about him, she left her office and headed toward the car. The evening ahead promised to be dreary and lonely. She had become accustomed to having company with dinner, and the prospect of dining alone depressed her. Meredith, in low spirits, tried to think of a way to cheer herself up. She would take a long bubble bath, then spend the evening shopping. The thought of a new dress, or a new anything for that matter, always lifted her spirits . . . at least a bit.

Meredith glanced at the clock, then stared back at the maze of paperwork covering her desk. The day had been endless. There was really not much to be done until the new prototype was delivered. Paperwork bored her. She stood up and paced around the office. Her life was in such a jumble it was hard to concentrate. She had lost a friend and lost the man she wanted more than anything else in life. But there had to be a way to turn things around and make them work for her. Shaking her head in disgust, she began stacking the papers and returning them to the proper files. Hearing footsteps, she looked up.

"It can't be," she said laughing. "Bea! What are you doing here?"

"Hello." Aero-Dynamics' petite blonde administrative assistant strolled inside. "It's vacation time for this overworked lady!"

"Boy, am I glad to see you! Let's go to the Officers' Club. I'll buy you a drink, then we can decide where to have dinner. That is, if you're free."

"Sure am and the Officers' Club sounds great. You know, things just haven't been the same back at the office since you left. I miss you!"

"Bea, believe me, I miss you too! The past few weeks have been really muddled and there's been no one to talk to here. Not in this sea of men!"

"I should have it so rough."

"I'm serious. Anyway, I've got some good news and some bad news. How about you?"

"Nothing's new in my life, sorry to say. Maybe after I finish vacation there'll be something. At least I'm hoping."

"Oh, I see. Footloose and fancy free?"

"Not for long, I hope. What I need is one of those romantic liaisons I'm always reading about in my torrid little novels."

"Who doesn't?"

"Let's go. We can have a couple of drinks, then paint the town. What do you say?"

"Sure!"

When they arrived at the club, they glanced around, hoping for a free table. As usual, after hours it was jammed. Bea spotted a small spot by the wall and led the way. Ordering a round for both of them, she settled back and relaxed. "Well, tell me about it. Who's new in your life and what's happening?"

Under Bea's gentle prodding, Meredith recounted the entire story from beginning to end. "That's about it. Now, I've got to figure out what I'm going to do, if anything."

"The first thing we should do is get off the base and have dinner in a civilian atmosphere. It looks like you've about had it with our noble warriors."

The women left their table and walked to the parking lot. The area, covered in darkness, was illuminated sporadically by the lights of passing cars.

Meredith stopped in mid stride as she heard hushed, familiar voices to her right. Placing her hand on Bea's arm, she signaled her friend to remain still. Keeping their voices deliberately low, Mike and Jeff engaged in a game of hard and vicious verbal sparring. Hearing her name being bandied about, Meredith clenched her jaw. It was bad enough the two could spew such venom, but using her as a tool against each other made her feel cheap. Slowly her fists clenched into a tight, hard ball.

"How's it feel to know your girl prefers me, Ryan?" Mike asked.

"I wasn't aware she did."

"I think you are. Now the shoe is on the other foot."

"For the last time, I had no idea Carey was your fiancée. I dated her a few times and that was all."

"You used her and pushed her out the door when you got tired of her."

"We've been over this."

"We're even now. Can't tell you how much that pleases me?"

"Drop it."

"Meredith is a pretty talented little gal."

Meredith continued to listen, entranced by the conversation. A cold chill seeped through her veins as a hard, calculating look came over her face.

"Yes, sir! I've got to hand it to her. She really knows how to please a man."

Meredith shook with rage. How dare they discuss her in those terms! To think she had trusted Mike! He was a liar as well as a creep. Edging closer, she caught a glimpse of the men fighting. Jeff's fist had crashed soundly into Mike's middle, leaving him gasping for air. Parrying, Mike struck a paralyzing blow to Jeff's jaw. Thrown a few steps backward, Jeff lunged forward. Meredith, quickly stepping out of the shadows, faced them both.

Both men stopped abruptly and stared at her. Her cheeks flashed shades of crimson as her anger surfaced. "Mike, you are beneath contempt. I never slept with you, and you know it. Why you use me as a tool in your fight with him is beyond me. If you thought he was such a bastard for taking your girl, then what does that make you? At least his motive wasn't revenge. Besides being a liar, you are a complete..." Meredith struggled, trying to find the right word. "Cockroach," she spat out.

Meredith glanced at Jeff. The cut on his cheek needed tending. Without thinking, she reached out to touch him. Abruptly, in a change of heart, she spun on her heel and walked toward her car, leaving the men behind her.

Inside the car, Bea reached for her friend in a gesture of compassion. "You're upset and it's understandable, but there's something you should be aware of."

Meredith looked at her friend, waiting for an explanation.

"You told me Jeff was in love with Nicole, but if that's true, why would he fight for you?"

"He wasn't fighting for me. He was fighting Mike, which he's been itching to do for a while."

"But what provoked his anger was jealousy over you, don't you see? Besides, Meri, you didn't see his face. When you walked toward him then changed your mind and walked away, you really took him by surprise. I think he was ready to come to you."

"Bea, maybe he was just curious."

"No, Meri. There was something in the way he looked at you. His eyes softened. I can't really explain it, but believe me, I didn't imagine it. It was there."

"Bea, I haven't the remotest idea what's going on."

"You told me that you saw him kissing the other girl, right?"

"Yes, that's when Mike took me out of the restaurant."

"Did you ever wonder about what you saw? Perhaps you missed a key part of the incident. She could have kissed him. He's just a man. Maybe he responded out of habit, then realized what was happening. You didn't stick around, so how would you know?"

"Bea, I'd like to believe that, but..."

"Look, Meri, underneath all your tough exterior you're a softy. And you're too damn insecure." Bea sat for a few minutes, deep in thought. "When you walked out with Mike, did Jeff come after you?"

"Oh...well, not right away."

"What happened. What did he say?"

"Nothing." Meredith made a face. "Actually, I

didn't give him much of a chance."

"Go on."

"Mike was with me and I guess . . . I blew it."

"So what are you going to do about it?"

"There's still Nicole."

"You don't know that. The point is, Meri, you're seeing another side to it. So now what? Will you just turn your back on the whole thing?"

"I just don't know. Bea, I'm going to have to think about it."

"Okay. I'll tell you what. Let's talk about it over dinner. Maybe we can sort things out. What do you say?"

"All right. That sounds fine. Should we go fancy or casual?"

Bea glanced down at the denim pantsuit she wore, then looked at Meredith. Following her gaze, both women began to laugh.

"Right," Meredith replied. "Casual it is."

Choosing a pizza parlor, Meredith and Bea, famished, walked directly to the salad bar. After the waitress brought them a large pizza, they ate greedily and soon the plate lay empty. Leaning back against their booths, they sipped their soft drinks.

"Meri, do you still love Jeff?"

"I wish to God I could say I didn't, but I love that man more than anything else."

"Why don't you talk to him tomorrow. I think you've foolishly jumped to conclusions in this situation. Maybe you can straighten things out, or at least you'll find out for sure where you stand."

"Tomorrow."

"I wouldn't put it off too long, Meri. He's an awfully attractive man. If he doesn't have something going with that other girl, there'll be plenty of others willing to take her place."

"Yes, I realize that, but there is a small problem. I may not even get to see him tomorrow. We're scheduled to start carrier ops."

"Huh?"

"Testing on the carrier. He'll leave early in the morning, or tonight. I have to stay on base and go out tomorrow with the rest of the engineers and maintenance personnel."

"You'll find a way. I know you, kiddo. When something means enough to you, you'll move heaven and earth to get it."

"It isn't that simple with this."

"I have confidence in you. Like I said, you're a very resourceful lady when the stakes are high."

Meredith looked pensive. "Well, at least one of us is confident."

The women returned to Bea's hotel after a brief sightseeing tour. Chatting until the early morning, they reluctantly decided it was time for their evening to end. Exhausted, they began their good-byes.

"Where to now, Bea?"

"I have about a week left of vacation time. I'm going to spend it driving along the coast and stopping wherever the fancy strikes me. I just want to relax and forget the office for a while."

"I'll call you and let you know what happened. Will you be back in Carmel next week?"

"Yes."

After one final hug, Meredith returned to her car. Talking to Bea had done her a world of good. There were times a woman needed another woman to talk to. Bea was a good friend. In fact, there were times when she was more like a sister.

Driving back to the hotel, Meredith's thoughts drifted to Jeff. There were no guarantees, but Bea had been right. She couldn't turn her back on the possibility. She *was* too insecure. Jeff meant too much.

And hadn't he shown his love and spoken of it often? Resolving to find time with him alone in the days to come, Meredith parked her car and walked to her room.

The thought of an encounter with Jeff excited her. If there was one chance in a million she had misjudged him, it was worth the gamble.

The following morning, Meredith arrived at her office an hour early. Jeff normally came in before anyone else, and she hoped for a few minutes alone before they reported on board. Hoping he hadn't left the night before, she paced back and forth, toying with her rings. When the noise of people filling the building reached her, she glanced down the corridor, hoping for a glimpse. When he failed to appear, she went in search of Bill. Finding him sipping coffee in his office, she smiled.

"Good morning. Have you seen Jeff?"

"Good morning, and he's gone. He'll meet us on board. He had some paperwork at headquarters to straighten out."

Meredith returned to her office. She was bitterly disappointed that their talk would have to be postponed. She was pressed to get her equipment together for the sea trials. Hurrying, she forced her thoughts to her work. Handing her suitcase and computer terminal to one of the sailors on duty, she checked over some specification sheets, then stuffed them inside her briefcase.

Outside, she searched for the jeep that was supposed to be waiting for her. Within seconds, the driver pulled up, stopping a few feet from her. "Ready, ma'am?"

"That's service!"

"That's what I'm here for."

As the sailor sped away, Meredith felt an odd sensation in the pit of her stomach. Despite the show of confidence she had put on for Jeff's benefit, she was not totally satisfied with the engineering department's decision to proceed. What if the second prototype malfunctioned? Trying to shake her worries, she reasoned silently that the others were undoubtedly right. Yet a nagging worry persisted. When they arrived at the dock, she caught her first sight of the carrier designated for the assignment. Despite the fact that it was supposed to be one of the smallest available, it seemed large enough to encompass a city.

She tried to radiate confidence as she walked across the gang plank. The sides, made up of rope, wobbled in the breeze, but the base was steady under their weight. As they stepped onto the deck, Meredith followed the young ensign through a doorway, then through a maze of gray corridors. The officer stopped at one of the doors and held it open for her. Meredith walked in, surprised at the austerity of the setting. Realizing the men lived in the metal cities for months at a time, she had expected something a little less monastic. The gray metal lockers stood bolted against the far wall, and a small sink was at the opposite wall. The rickety cot that was to be her bed was bolted down to the floor, ensuring its stability during heavy seas.

Meredith turned to ask the ensign about the bathrooms and showers, but he had already gone. Hanging up the few things she had brought along, Meredith started searching for the other engineers. Following the voices echoing down the corridor, she reached the recreation area. Several men sat around the room playing cards. Immediately aware of her presence, an enlisted man came to her assistance.

"Ma'am, we're shoving off in a few minutes. Can I show you how to get back on the dock?"

Meredith, bestowing her best icy stare, responded evenly. "I belong here, mister. I'm to oversee the testing of the Scorpio, so if you would point in the direction of the pilot's ready room, I would appreciate it."

The man, obviously taken aback, stammered as he gave her the directions. As Meredith returned to the hallway, she heard the exchange going on between the men. They simply would have to get used to her, she thought with a grin. Besides, if they didn't like women on board, that was their problem, not hers.

Hoping to come across Jeff, Meredith walked to the pilot's ready room. Gear lay neatly hung on hooks, and maps were taped to the tables. Unable to find anyone, she hesitated.

Shrugging her shoulders, she left and started for the stairs. She climbed up, in search of the flight deck somewhere above. Cautiously opening a set of double doors, she smiled and stepped outside. Men dressed in bright blues and yellows milled about the floating airfield. She was reminded of the giant ants in the late-night horror shows as they moved about in tightly fitted helmets that completely covered their features. The Scorpio, ready for testing, stood at the far side of the deck. Crew members surrounded her, busily checking over her instruments.

When Meredith joined them, she heard a ripple of sounds behind her. Taking care not to show hesitation, she took control, carefully directing the checks. It was a beautiful morning. The carrier began edging out to the open seas while she designated tasks to the crew men. The breeze, although slightly chilly, was not unpleasant. Her ski jacket offered enough protection, keeping her comfortable.

The morning passed quickly. As the time for the first catapult launch neared, Meredith caught her first glimpse of Jeff. Helmet in hand, he stood by one of the plane captains, signing some papers. Meredith began to walk toward him, then, changing her mind, climbed up the tower the men had coined Vulture's Row. She would oversee testing from that vantage point.

Walking briskly across the windswept deck, Jeff stopped a few feet from the Scorpio. Giving his plane captain a snappy salute, he waited for the crew man to jump down onto the flight deck. Circling the aircraft slowly, he began the age-old ritual of wiggling this and probing that, glancing critically at everything about the prototype. Finished, he smiled and nodded. With confidence mirrored in his every move, he climbed aboard and eased himself down into the cockpit.

Meredith felt her stomach tighten in anticipation. Everything had to go according to plan. If anything went wrong, he would crash into the ocean. Without enough time to eject, the outcome would be certain.

The flight deck was soon filled with the thunderous sounds of the twin-jet engines. Slowly the Scorpio taxied, edging out to the starboard catapult. Crew members hooked up the hold-back cables while Jeff went through some rapid checks. The catapult officer, pointing directly at the noonday sun, began to twirl his finger, and Jeff throttled the jets to full power. The Scorpio bucked and strained against the cables that held it securely in place. Meredith saw Jeff give a quick thumbs-up signal to the officer on deck.

The officer waited, concentrating on the pitch of the deck. The shot had to be timed perfectly. As the bow settled downward, just prior to its upward swing, the officer snapped his arm outward. The Scorpio slammed forward and shot up into the air.

The speaker crackled alive, and the sound of Jeff's voice could be heard plainly in the tower. "Shangri-la, this is *Red Dog One*. How do you read me?"

"Read you loud and clear."

"Test sequence Alpha completed satisfactorily. Progressing to next sequence."

"Roger."

Meredith watched breathlessly as Jeff placed the Scorpio through a series of maneuvers. Jeff banked his aircraft to port side and into a shallow dive. Slowly the Scorpio leveled off. Cutting in the afterburners, he began a steep climb. As he faded from view, disappearing into the clouds, the crew waited. A ray of sunlight hit the canopy and a faint gleam was seen dropping from the sky like a falling star. Leveling off just below the base of a cloud, he began to climb again, forming a tight inside loop. The test finished with a series of port and starboard rolls. Completing the last slow turn, he lined up the plane with the carrier.

Meredith edged closer to the speaker. "Shangri-la, this is *Red Dog One*."

"Come in, *Red Dog One*."

"Have finished check-off list. Request permission to begin recovery-and-arrest sequence."

"Roger. Permission granted. Begin your approach."

Jeff was circling the carrier. Meredith closed her eyes and pictured Jeff making his preparations for touchdown. Eyes glued to the light-framed mirror on the deck of the carrier, he would watch for the amber ball, dubbed the "meatball."

As he began his descent, he remembered the basics that had been carefully ingrained in his memory. The meatball would alert him only if he was coming in at the wrong angle. It wouldn't help him at all if he drifted off to one side. Keeping the yellow center line of the deck lined up with his aircraft, he would adjust his air speed, keeping it at 80 percent full power. When he felt the Scorpio slam against the deck, he would wonder if the hook had caught the arresting cable. Automatically he would push the throttle to full military power. The standard safety procedure would ensure enough speed to take off again in case of a miss. Meredith opened her eyes. Catching the wire at about 140 miles per hour, the Scorpio looked as though a giant invisible hand had whacked and held it. As the crew came rushing out, Jeff accepted his plane captain's help to get out of the cockpit and scramble off the plane.

Meredith could see he was exhilarated. Everything had gone perfectly. Later, after his report had been filed, she would find time alone with him. He would still be basking in the excitement of a job well done and would be more receptive to her.

Leaving the tower, or the island, as they called it, she walked directly to the ready room. She was eager to see him, if only for a second. He was facing away from her, talking to another pilot.

"Jeff!" she called softly.

He turned around and gave her an arrogant grin. Walking toward her, he stood deliberately close. "Your fighter did well. I'll file a full report within the hour."

"Yes, I'm glad it performed well for you, but I'd like to talk to you."

"I'm listening, but are you sure you don't want me to start working on that report while everything's still fresh in my mind?"

Meredith, annoyed, pursed her lips. "Yes, of course. We wouldn't want to tax your memory."

Angrily, she whirled around and began to walk out of the room, but Jeff's hand stopped her, then pulled her around to face him. "What were you going to say?"

"Nothing at all," she replied coldly.

"Does this mean I won't get any adulation from you?"

"Sure. I'm going to rush out and buy you a gold star."

"I prefer other methods of reward."

"Back to that, are we?" Meredith replied with a sly grin. "Well, fella, there are plenty of cute guys around, I want ya to know."

Quickly Jeff pulled her aside. "Don't even kid that way in here!"

"Oh, I see," she whispered. "A closet type."

"Meri, damn it!"

"Meet me later in my cabin."

"Now, you're talking!"

Meredith walked toward the door, then turned around. Smiling, she looked him over, moving her gaze with deliberate slowness up and down his body. "No, never mind. You can't read your instruction manual in the dark."

Leaving him open mouthed and red faced, she closed the door.

# - 10 -

HOURS LATER, MEREDITH paced impatiently in the small cabin. Perhaps she had teased him too much. If he had decided not to show, she would have lost one of the best days for a serious talk with him. Smiling, she shook her head. There were times it was difficult to be serious around him. Hearing a knock, Meredith leaped from her chair.

"I'm glad you came!"

"You knew I would." Stepping inside, he stopped and faced her. "Didn't you?"

Meredith shrugged. "I wasn't sure. But now that you're here, I want to apologize for our misunderstanding. I . . . I was a fool to believe you were two-timing me with Nicole."

"No, it wasn't your fault. I should have tried to make you see that—"

Meredith laughed. "Who cares? It's behind us now. Commander, may I say you look absolutely sensational in a flight suit?"

"Thanks," he replied with a sheepish grin.

"At least it bulges where you don't."

"Damn you, Meri." Pulling her against him, he kissed her savagely. His lips molded her mouth, forcing it to part. Meredith struggled to get her breath, but his arms held her steady. Her lips bruised under the fierceness of his desire. His tongue tasted hers in a kiss so possessive it drained her strength. Leaning against him for support, she matched his passion, eager to seal their union.

"I suppose you know what this means," he said, easing his hold.

"Sure," she said, pushing away from him. "You crave my nubile young body."

"That too. Marriage plans back on?"

"Of course."

"Meri, it's about time!" he whispered, taking her into his arms once again. "Look, Nicole is my past. You are my present and my future. Don't ever forget, you desirable witch!"

"Now you're talking!" Leaping into his arms, she laughed. As he caught her, Jeff fell backward, onto the cot. "What wonderful timing you have, sweet stuff. This is just where I was heading myself."

Meredith managed to get away and look at him in horror. "Not here!"

"But why not? If you'll keep the light on, I can glance at the instruction manual from time to time."

"I hope your manual has *lots* of pages. I'd get tired of the same old thing day after day."

"Tired? Same old thing?" Jeff echoed in mock outrage. He pulled her back on the cot and pinned her down with one hand while he tickled her unmercifully with the other. "Say you're sorry and that you'll be my obedient slave from this day on."

"I'd rather die!" she said, laughing.

Jeff stopped and looked at her tenderly. "Why do

I get the feeling I'm going to have my hands full with you?"

Meredith stood up and straightened her clothing. "Well, at least life won't be boring."

Taking her by the hand, Jeff led her to the door. "Come with me."

Meredith followed, silently enjoying the firmness of his grip as they walked down a cramped corridor. Stopping by one of the rooms, he pulled the door open and invited her inside. Closing the door with his foot, he waved a complacent hand around the room.

"My lair."

"Jeff, really! They'll miss us."

Jeff chuckled. "Now who's got a one-track mind! Wait a second." Reaching inside his suitcase, he brought out a small velvet box. Meredith recognized it at once.

"My ring," she whispered.

"Yes. I've kept it with me every day. You see, I knew it was just a matter of time."

Meredith inched closer to him. Slipping her hands inside his flight suit, she caressed with infinite sureness the rippling flesh inside. Jeff's arms automatically wrapped around her waist, bringing her closer. As she pressed her cheek against the thick mat of hair on his chest, she felt her body come fully alive with desire. Pushing back slightly, he brought his lips down to meet hers. Meredith felt his muscles tighten in response to the long, deep kiss.

Taking a step backward, she smiled. "Phew!"

"Celibacy seems destined to become one of my virtues for a while, whether I like it or not," Jeff commented.

"Don't feel bad."

"You wouldn't know any quick remedies, would you?"

"Me? You're the one with all the experience."

"Well, yes. That is true."

"Watch it, buster. You're expected to protest."

"Why? I'm not the one who's supposed to wear white on the wedding day, you know. In fact, grooms, Navy ones at least, wear black."

Meredith cocked her head, eyes sparkling with mischief. "Are you about to confess your many transgressions during your years of service to Uncle Sam?"

"We *are* ambassadors of good will. . . ."

"Forgive the pun, but you're leading me to believe I should have you altered after the wedding."

He guffawed. "But, Meredith, that's self-punishment!"

"Darn right," she said quickly. She broke the gaze between them and started combing her hair in front of a small mirror ontt he wall. Then her eyes focused on the clock. "Jiminy Christmas! I'm supposed to be going over some details on the Scorpio test. I've got to get going! Are you coming?"

Jeff turned away. "No. I'll be along later."

"Uh huh." Meredith grinned, then turned him around. Slowly glancing down his body, she gave him a sly look. "Yes, and maybe a cold shower would help."

"Out!" Leading her toward the door, he gave her a gentle push into the hallway. "Get going," he growled, rapping her playfully on the rear.

In high spirits, Meredith walked to the hangar deck. Seeing the Scorpio surrounded by technicians, she strolled toward it. The team of specialists were carefully measuring performance level and recording data, feeding information to the computer back on shore. A careful record had to be kept and constant monitoring was required at this stage.

For the next few days, Meredith seldom had a chance to see Jeff alone. The Scorpio's performance had been excellent; everyone was talking about the new fighter. Its capabilities had been enhanced by a few modifications, and the new prototype seemed to delight in the challenge. The test pilots involved in the trials wrote glowing reports. Still, something nagged at the back of her mind. Something wasn't quite right, but she couldn't put her finger on it. Working round the clock, she pressed the mechanics for more tests and more data for the computers. Her reputation as a taskmaster was clearly spreading throughout the ship, and she began to notice that several of the men were avoiding her.

Late one evening in her room, as she poured over the latest findings, a knock sounded. Meredith answered the door, edging it open carefully. Jeff, with his warm, boyish grin, framed the doorway.

"Hi there! Come in."

Jeff stepped inside. "I haven't seen you in two days. Are you trying to set a record or just impress the hell out of everyone with how hard you work?"

"Jeff, it's the Scorpio malfunction. I know everyone concluded it was a factory error, but I can't shake the feeling there's something we're missing."

"Sweetheart, look. We've flown it and if there had been something wrong, it would have cropped up by now. I think you may be overly concerned about my safety, and that's what's causing your doubts."

"Perhaps, but I'm usually not wrong about things like this. My instincts are pretty reliable. I have the worst feeling we're courting disaster."

"You are, but it has nothing to do with the Scorpio. Not directly, anyway. Meredith, do you realize just how hard you've been riding the men? All I ever seem to hear is what a battle ax you've become."

"I'm sorry they feel that way, but there's a lot that

needs to be done. Besides, Jeff, what they think of me really doesn't matter. I know there's something staring me right in the face and I can't see it!"

"Do you have to become such a shrew to find it?"

"Is that what you think of me? I'm a shrew?"

"Well, you haven't exactly been charming lately."

"And I suppose everyone under your command is absolutely in love with you."

"That's different."

"How? We've both a job to do. If they don't like me, it hardly matters."

"My job demands their obedience, Meri. Men don't always accept that easily."

"Exactly."

"Your job doesn't entail the same thing."

"I haven't gone out of my way to be pleasant. However, I haven't been rude, either. That is until now, particularly if you insist on having this conversation."

"So what you're saying is that you're going to do whatever you please, regardless of what I say."

"I don't tell you how to do your job, so don't tell me how to do mine."

Jeff glared at her, his eyes flashing. Their eyes locked in a silent struggle as each tried to assert dominance over the other. "Sometimes you can be so damned stubborn!" he whispered.

Crossing the room with large, confident strides, Jeff grasped her arm. In one fluid motion he pushed her robe down over her shoulders. Meredith, angered by his attitude and actions, stood her ground, eyes blazing with a fiery rage. Before she had a chance to speak, his mouth covered hers with a roughness and possessiveness she found hard to resist.

Releasing her slightly, Jeff smiled. "Now give me a chance to explain what I mean. It's to your own advantage."

"Jeff, do your job and let me do mine," she responded, trying to keep her breathing even.

Jeff's eyes fell softly over the contours of her body. He started to speak, but then, with a gesture of resignation, turned and left, closing the door lightly behind him.

Meredith adjusted her robe and wrapped it snuggly about her. With a smug smile, she returned to her desk. He'd just have to learn that she would never allow him to use her love for him as a weapon against her.

The next morning, when the men saw her come onto the hangar deck, silent glances were exchanged. Meredith, aware of the reaction her presence evoked, resolved to be more patient but not to compromise the amount of work she required from them. She might even be able to get more from them if she made an effort to keep her temper in check.

The morning passed quickly as tests were carried out and repeated. The aircraft performed well, responding to the slightest commands from its pilot. As they lowered it back onto the hangar deck, Meredith began to complete the checklist on her clipboard. Strolling toward the candy machines, called the Gedunk Shoppe for some unfathomable reason, she stopped, curious about the conversation in the next room.

"That lady engineer isn't half bad now that she's quit pushing so hard."

"Maybe she had some personal problem. You're no picnic either when your wife hassles you, you know."

"She ain't married."

"So? Maybe it was something else. Who knows? I'll tell you something, though, if she acts as nice as she did this morning, I'll work overtime whenever she wants."

Meredith chuckled softly. It was better this way. As her mind returned to the scene with Jeff the previous night, the grin turned into a scowl. When the men's new resolve reached his ears, as it undoubtedly would, he'd be totally insufferable!

She would have to convince him that it had been her own decision and not one due to his caveman act. That somehow threatened to be a monumental task.

As the day progressed, Meredith grew more and more pleased by the work the mechanics were accomplishing. They seemed more receptive and eager to help. After the final checks were completed, Meredith returned to her room. Tired, she lay on her cot and closed her eyes. She would be glad when they reached land again. She desperately wanted to return to Carmel and give the computers one last chance to locate the problem they had encountered in the original prototype.

She needed to find a concrete reason for the Scorpio's malfunction, one that would satisfy her. One thing she had learned through experience was that malfunctions don't simply disappear. She was genuinely concerned over Jeff's safety. If a factory error had been the problem, it was possible that it was only temporarily obscured in the new prototype. The only way to solve the riddle and put her mind at rest would be to spend about four hours with the main computer. If nothing showed up then, she would accept the decision of the others.

Hungry, Meredith walked to the Officers' Lounge in search of something to eat. Cold cuts were kept in the refrigerator, along with all the other makings of a sandwich.

After preparing a snack, she sat on the couch and read a novel she had purchased a few days before. Annoyed by its tendency to close shut, she anchored her knee against it.

When Jeff wandered in, Meredith, engrossed in her book, paid no attention. Creeping across the room, he sat by her side and waited.

Meredith, startled, looked up. "Do you always pop in like that?"

Jeff grinned. "No. Sometimes I take my time and do it right."

Meredith closed her eyes and opened them again. "Here we go. Another stroll down gutter lane."

"Sorry. Couldn't pass it up. By the way, I'm glad you decided to do as I said."

Meredith stared blankly at him. "What are you babbling about?"

"You've stopped acting like such a shrew around the men."

"If you think my change of heart was due to your dubious charm, you're flattering yourself. I had decided, long before you said anything, I could get more work out of the men this way."

Jeff chuckled. "Uh huh. Whatever you say."

Meredith glared at him. She spun on her heel and headed for the door. Before she had a chance to get far, Jeff pulled her toward him. Prepared for his move, she retaliated, hurling him over hip in a classic judo throw.

Jeff fell to the deck with a dull thud, his eyes wide with amazement. "You could have done that anytime before!"

Meredith tilted her head to one side. A smile touched the corners of her mouth. "That's right. I have a brown belt in judo."

Trying not to laugh, she sauntered out of the room, gracefully swaying her hips.

## - *11* -

THE FOLLOWING AFTERNOON the giant carrier edged
up to the docks. Testing had been a success and Aero-
Dynamics was assured a sizable contract for the
fighter. Only one task remained. The base commander
had scheduled a flight demonstration for NATO VIPs
due on base the following day. Before the Scorpio's
display, Meredith would fly to Carmel and go through
one final computer check. The catapult mechanism
could have hidden the elusive malfunction, she was
taking no chances with Jeff's life.

On board she had managed to devise a plan that
would eliminate all doubts once and for all. Program-
ming all the design specifications and modifications
on the Scorpio that had existed from day one into the
master computer, she would isolate each system and
trace the causes of the loss of power.

Gathering her things, Meredith toyed with an idea.

Perhaps the malfunction was caused by a component slipping in and out of place. That would explain a lot! But how could she ever find something that erratic! Her only hope lay in long hours with the computer in Carmel.

Meredith carried the small suitcase off the ship. Tossing it casually into the back of the jeep, she motioned to the driver. "I'm in a hurry."

Meredith glanced at her watch. She had to make sure the company plane would be ready for her. As soon as the jeep stopped, Meredith jumped out. Grabbing her suitcase, she walked to her car and placed it on the back seat. Time was at a premium. She dashed to her office and placed a call. The Cessna would be fueled and waiting. Meredith locked her office. As she turned the corner, she saw Jeff.

"Oh, I'm glad to see you," she stammered. "I don't have time to explain, but I'm going back to Carmel. I'll be back tomorrow."

Meredith hesitated, curbing the impulse to ask that the flight demonstration be postponed. Realizing he would never consent, particularly since he felt she was being overprotective, she gave him a quick good-bye kiss. "I'll be back as soon as I can."

Racing to her car, she sped away from the base. Since the problem had only surfaced during airfield takeoffs, there was a chance she would be able to pin it down eventually. If only they hadn't scheduled the air show for the following day! What she needed most—and lacked—was time.

Arriving at a private airstrip, Meredith received the necessary weather information and jogged to the plane. Her stomach felt tied in knots. Time was slipping past her and there was no way to slow it down. Starting the engines, she checked all the gauges and taxied down the runway. Building up her speed, she felt the landing gear lose contact with the ground.

Pointing the nose up, she climbed until she reached cruising altitude.

Meredith inhaled softly. There was an incredible amount of work to be done before morning. She would have to spend an all-nighter at the computer annex with pots of steaming hot coffee. Well, it wouldn't be the first time. The minute she had what she needed she would return to San Diego. If by early tomorrow morning she had not found anything, she would be ready to concede. Since the demonstration was not scheduled until eleven-thirty in the morning, she would have ample time to return. Thinking of the long night ahead of her, Meredith sighed.

Her trip was slow and uneventful. Anticipation added to her mounting tension. She was glad when she reached the company's landing strip a few hours later. Maneuvering the airplane, she reduced her airspeed and made a perfect landing. As she stepped out of the airplane, she waved to one of the mechanics and ran toward her car. The men always parked it inside the hangar whenever she left on extended business trips.

As she drove to the computer building inside the complex, Meredith prayed silently. Why couldn't she shake that premonition of disaster?

Stopping by Bea's desk, Meredith greeted her friend. "Hi! I'm glad you're back. I haven't got time to explain or talk, but bring the biggest pot of coffee you can get to the annex. Also, please make sure that I'm not disturbed. I've got a deadline."

"You got it."

Meredith walked across the courtyard and entered the building at the rear. The room was filled, wall to wall, with huge memory banks and components. Sitting by the typewriter link, Meredith banged her fist against the desk. She had forgotten to pick up the specs on the Scorpio. Startled by a noise behind her, she spun in her chair. Bea, balancing a large number of documents in her arms, dropped them unceremoniously on the desk.

"I may be wrong, but if all this has to do with the Scorpio Project, you're going to need these. I'll get the rest together and bring them to you."

"Bea, you're an angel! I was in such a rush, I forgot."

Sifting through the documents, Meredith began the slow, painstaking process. The hours passed, and the only thing she had gained was a headache. Cursing silently, she stepped outside for a breath of fresh air. When the door to the main building swung open, Bea stepped out, carrying a sandwich and a glass of milk.

"Good! You're taking a break. You've been working for six hours straight. If you have something to eat, you'll be in better shape to continue."

"You sound like a mother hen, and thanks. You can't believe how discouraging this is. I can't find what I'm looking for, and I just know there's something I'm overlooking!"

"You're the best engineer this firm has. If there's a problem, you'll find it."

"With time I could, but that's just it. There isn't any."

"Take a break. Afterward maybe you'll be better able to spot whatever it is."

Meredith aimlessly nibbled at her sandwich. Discouragement and fear plagued her attempts to remain cool. As she stared into space, an idea took shape in her mind.

Meredith ran inside the building. Typing data furiously into the terminal, she sat back and waited. The computer made its usual clicking and humming sounds, but no answer came. Her prodding only resulted in the monitor flashing the word WORKING.

Meredith paced around the room. Finally, she heard the familiar clicking and a reply was printed before her.

Meredith read the printout over and over again in disbelief. It had been so simple! Why hadn't she thought of it? A valve, intermittently malfunctioning in the fuel system, would cause the engines to loose power occasionally. The erratic sticking might not have shown up in their tests but could reappear at any time, unless the problem was corrected. They had been lucky so far, but next time . . .

Meredith looked at her watch. Eight o'clock. If she returned to San Diego right away, she would have time to get some sleep and still arrive early at work tomorrow. Providing the repairs could be done quickly, the demonstration could proceed as scheduled.

Meredith packed up the printouts and drove to the landing strip. She was glad her flight would not have to be rushed. She enjoyed flying at night. The masses of twinkling lights were a spectacular sight.

Meredith parked her car in its customary space and walked toward the airplane. Checking to make sure it had been refueled and all was ready, she started the engines. After receiving the signal from the tower, she eased the throttle forward and began her ascent. Enjoying the peacefulness of the skies around her, she sat back and relaxed. Everything was working according to plan. The tests were nearing their end, and before long she would be Mrs. Jeff Ryan. The name echoed silently in her ears.

At first, distracted by daydreams, she ignored the slight turbulence. As she pressed on, Meredith felt it grow worse. Reproaching herself for not checking the weather reports, she concentrated on the instruments. The high winds began to buffet the small plane, whipping it to and fro. With adrenalin surging through her, she veered toward the mountains. The storm seemed to be coming from the sea. Perhaps if she strayed farther inland, she would be able to bypass it. Meredith diverted her route toward the Santa Ana Mountains. As the storm increased its fury, she uttered an oath. A mounting fear replaced her earlier complacency. Her stomach tightened into a knot as she tried to see ahead. Lightning flashed all around her.

Meredith swallowed, trying to aid her dry throat. She had to do something. Perspiration dripped freely from her forehead. Reaching for the receiver, she began to switch from frequency to frequency. No reply came through any of the channels. Realizing her own impending danger, she made the decision to land. If she stayed in the air, it would not be long before a strong gust tossed her into a mountainside, killing her on impact. Landing would be hazardous, but at least she would have a chance.

Dropping below the base of the cloud, she tried to pick out a clearing in the forest. In the darkness, the terrain below was an ominous expanse of black. To drop her altitude any more would increase the chances of running into the high treetops she knew were below. Her only hope lay in timing a landing with the series of brief but frequent lightning flashes around her. After a few minutes had elapsed, Meredith began to doubt she'd ever find someplace to land.

Circling slowly, she searched for suitable spot. In a desperate gamble, she descended, edging dangerously close to the ground. As lightning pierced the blackness surrounding her, Meredith spotted a road. Exhaling loudly, she struggled for another glimpse. The thin strip would serve as her runway. Lining up her approach, she began to slow her airspeed. Seeing the ground come toward her at frightening speed,

Meredith cut power to the engines, running the small aircraft close to stalling speed. If she stalled completely, she'd crash. But if she came in too quickly, the airplane would break up. Taking a deep breath, she braced herself for the impact. When she touched the ground, Meredith felt herself being thrown forward. The landing gear had been sucked into the mud. Praying no cars were nearby, she fought to keep the airplane upright as it jerked and fishtailed violently. Suddenly the left wing tangled in the branch of a tree, hurling the plane off the road and down the side of an embankment. Her head crashed against the wheel. A blinding flash of light exploded before her, then everything turned black.

Meredith opened her eyes slowly, aware of an excrutiating pain. Only a faint glimmer of sunshine penetrated the fog around the airplane. Rubbing her eyes, she leaned back. Her vision seemed unwilling to cooperate. Closing her eyes, she waited a few seconds, hoping to ease the throbbing inside her skull. With an effort, she tried to focus on the hands of her watch. She had failed. The demonstration would go on in another hour unless she could get through and warn them.

Picking up the receiver, she switched to the military frequency. In a barely audible voice she began transmitting. "Mayday. This is CU 160. I've been forced down approximately ten miles north of Banner Peak. Project Scorpio demonstration is to be cancelled. Repeat. Cancelled. Do you read?"

The static sounds from the receiver crackled alive. "CU 160. Repeat message. Your transmission is faint. Only first part of message received. Repeat. Over."

Meredith pressed the speaker button. Sitting up, she felt a wave of nausea overcome her. Everything in front of her turned black, and she lapsed into un-consciousness.

Groggy, Meredith rubbed her aching forehead. She heard voices shouting. One gave a whoop and let out, "She's alive."

"Of course I'm alive," Meredith muttered. "But damn cold and with a terrible headache. So don't yell in my ear."

Meredith smiled thinly as Jeff approached. "I've never been so glad to see anyone in my life," she said.

Jeff wrapped his arms around her. "The feeling is mutual. Besides your head, are you hurt anywhere?"

"No. I banged my head pretty hard against the instruments, but otherwise I'm in good shape."

Lifting her easily in his arms, he began to carry her back to the jeep while Bill ran ahead. Meredith protested but to no avail.

"Shut up and enjoy it," he growled.

"I'm glad my message got through and you didn't take the Scorpio up."

"We got a message, but no one was quite sure of what you said. You didn't really think I'd go through with a demo when you were missing, did you?"

"Thank God you didn't. You were right. There was something wrong with the Scorpio. Jeff, ground the plane until I get a chance to work on it. Do you understand?"

"Yes. No one is going to fly it, so keep quiet and relax."

"I could walk."

"Meredith do you love me?"

"You know I do!"

"Then for the love of me and heaven, too, shut up!"

When they reached the road, Bill pulled up the jeep, stopping a few feet from them. Setting Meredith in the back seat, Jeff edged in beside her.

"Okay, Bill. We're ready. Head for the base."

"Why are we going to the base now? Can't you take me to my hotel? I'd like to take a hot bath and go to bed."

"I want the doctor to check you out first."

"Jeff, I'm fine. Let's go to the hotel. Really, I'm just tired."

Ignoring her protests, Jeff signaled his companion to drive to the base hospital. As they walked in, nurses immediately offered assistance. Placing a disgruntled Meredith into a wheelchair, they took her to one of the examine rooms. A nurse helped her undress while they waited for the physician to arrive. After a thorough check, he pronounced her sound.

The doctor stepped out into the corridor and gave Jeff the good news. As Meredith walked out to meet them, Jeff grinned and gave her a playful wink. "Doc, how about taking a couple of blood tests?"

"She doesn't need one, Commander." The doctor paused, then, catching his meaning, smiled. "Oh, one of those! You should have said so."

Blook samples taken, Meredith walked to the front entrance. Pulling up in his own car, Bill swung the door open for them. "I'll take you both to the hotel, then I'll bring you back here, Jeff, so you can pick up your car."

When they arrived at the hotel, Jeff helped Meredith to her room while Bill waited in the car downstairs.

Once inside her room, Meredith took two steps and bounced onto the bed. Waving good-bye to Jeff, she grinned.

"I'm not even going to change. I'm just going to sleep right here."

"I could help you change. After all, I'll be your husband in just a few days."

Meredith smiled as if toying with the idea. "I think I'll make you wait. Good night, Commander."

Jeff leaned over gently and kissed her. "I was so worried about you. Don't ever do that to me again!"

"I'll certainly try not to."

Jeff smiled. "Tomorrow we're getting married."

"What's this, another proposal?"

"No. Think of it as a promise."

"Jeff..."

"Don't argue."

Turning, he closed the door behind him. Meredith, feeling safe and at peace, closed her eyes and fell into a deep sleep.

# - 12 -

MEREDITH AWOKE EARLY the next morning. After a long bath and a hearty breakfast, she felt fully refreshed and decided to report to work. The repairs on the Scorpio still needed to be completed. Perhaps there would still be time for an air demonstration.

Meredith dressed carefully, wanting to look especially nice on her last day on the job. The Scorpio would finally be ready; her task would be at an end. After selecting a pair of black pants and a white V-neck sweater, she tied a royal blue scarf around her neck. Brushing her hair until it glistened, she allowed it to remain loose around her shoulders. As she studied her reflection, she nodded, pleased with the results.

Filled with anticipation, she drove to the base. She had been through a lot, but the future was filled with promise.

She parked the car in her usual spot and went directly into the hangar. The men turned around as she sauntered in, and two wolf whistles echoed out from somewhere in the back. Suppressing a grin, she walked upstairs to her office. Before the morning was through, a simple alteration on the faulty valve had been completed and the prototype was ready for its last test flight.

Jeff, returning from a morning conference, passed by her office and stopped abruptly. "What are you doing here?"

"I work here, remember?" Inviting him to sit down, with a careless wave of her hand, she continued. "I've called the base commander. The flight demo's on for this afternoon. Here's your chance to prove what a hot stick-and-rudder man you really are."

"You doubt it?"

"No, sir. But I must admit I'm more impressed by your other talents."

"Speaking of that, I've arranged for a justice of the peace to perform a ceremony at five this afternoon. What do you say?"

"Heavens! How nice of you to consult me on the time!"

"Well?"

"Oh, I think I'll be free then."

Jeff kicked the door shut with his foot and pulled her toward him, tickling her sides until she was helpless with laughter. "Will you be a good girl and stop giving me a hard time?"

Meredith tried to wiggle away, but Jeff reached for her side once more. "Oh, stop! Please. Yes, I'll be good."

"That's better," he said, releasing her.

Moving away from him, she straightened her sweater. "You better get going." She pointed to the clock on her wall. "You'll be late."

When Jeff left, Meredith sat down and began last-minute wrap-ups on her paperwork. Looking up, she leaned back on her chair. Her eyes wandered around the room and stopped at the clock. Losing trace of time was becoming one of her specialties. Running, Meredith left the building.

Jogging across the concrete runway, she headed toward the flight line. A handful of dignitaries stood nearby. Jeff saluted his plane captain and then climbed aboard the Scorpio. While the powerful jets thundered, Jeff checked off his final preflight procedures and pulled the throttle forward, summoning all the power into the engines. In a burst of acceleration, he was airborne.

Meredith watched as he put the fighter through its paces. He would slow down until the craft nearly lost power, then flash away with a roar. Jeff maneuvered the sleek aircraft, pushing it to its limits. As he entered the base of a cloud, the plane disappeared from sight. With the speed of lightning the aircraft reappeared, hurdling toward the earth in a spin. Meredith felt the contents of her stomach touch the back of her throat. A few hundred feet above the ground, Jeff pulled out of the dive in a graceful, easy style.

Meredith, pale, walked toward the ground-control vehicle where technicians were monitoring Jeff's radio communications. Jeff's voice crackled out of the speaker. "This aerial demonstration has been brought to you courtesy of Uncle Sam's best."

Meredith felt a twinge of anger. He had almost given her heart failure with his showing off. What the heck did he think he was doing? Fighting an impulse to snatch the receiver away from the operator, she resolved to give him a piece of her mind as soon as he landed.

"Thanks for the demonstration, *Scorpio Two*. Return to base."

*"Rajah!"*

When Meredith heard the southern drawl all pilots affected, she chuckled, despite herself. Even a simple response like *roger* would become *rajah* when the men were up in the air. Jeff was part of a breed that took risks for a living. To change or even try to modify him would never work. Perhaps that was one of the things that had attracted her to him. The incredible self-confidence and the subtle arrogance all went with the job. It would be part of the parcel that came with being Mrs. Jeff Ryan. Shaking her head, Meredith smiled to no one in particular.

As the aircraft approached the end of the field, she prepared to greet him. Instead of touching down, however, he buzzed the field at treetop level, then climbed full throttle vertically toward the clouds.

*"Scorpio Two,* let's have a demonstration of a landing sequence."

*"Rajah."*

Meredith laughed softly, seeing the little boy in the man. The base commander turned to the NATO officials and mumbled something about high-spirited fighter jocks, then quickly escorted them inside his waiting car.

As they walked past Meredith, the captain paused, then came toward her. "Tell your man that he should thank his wings that today's his wedding day. Otherwise, I'd ship his tail to Guam for the stunts he pulled here today."

Meredith grinned. "Thank you. I'd hate to honeymoon alone."

The officer nodded and, without another word, turned and joined his companions. Meredith breathed a sigh of relief.

This time the fighter made a normal landing and taxied up to the flight line. Meredith, deciding against a gentle rebuff, waited for him to emerge. The practical jokes and stunts were all a part of him, and she would accept him as he was. All she knew was that she loved him and that nothing would ever change that.

Meredith waited until he scrambled out of the cockpit. His face revealed the reaction of a little boy who knew he'd been bad but wouldn't get punished.

"You about gave me cardiac arrest," she said.

"Aw, I had everything under control."

Meredith rolled her eyes, and fell into step beside him as he looped his arm about her shoulders.

"Hey, it's almost time," he said. "Let me take a shower and change. I'll be with you in a few minutes." With a mischievous gleam in his eye, he added, "unless you want to join me; we could dry each other off."

Meredith poked him in the ribs. "Go take your shower. And make it a cold one!"

Returning to her office for the last time, she cleaned out her desk. The Scorpio Project had ended successfully. From now on she would work in the company's San Diego branch. Yes, things had turned out fine. She was scheduled to begin another government project at the end of the month, but she would have three weeks leave before having to report to work.

When Jeff strolled into her office, wearing his dress uniform, Meredith gave him a thorough appraisal. "Do I get a chance to dress up too?"

"Sure. Shall I drive you back to the hotel?"

"Nope. But you can meet me there in about an hour."

Meredith returned to her room and, after a bath, decided to wear the pale aqua dress she had been saving for a special occasion. Putting the finishing touches on her hair, she stood and walked to the door. By now, Jeff's knock had become a familiar and welcome sound.

After a short private ceremony inside the Officers'

Club, Jeff and his bride began the drive to the mountain cabin. Meredith felt excitement envelope her as she anticipated what was to come. The feeling, not needing to be suppressed, was intoxicating yet frightening. She allowed her eyes to focus on him. How handsome he was! His muscular chest and strong hands intensified the burning desire that was quickly spreading through her.

The car was curiously silent as each thought of the events leading up to the moment. When they arrived at the mountain home, Jeff stepped out of the car and lifted her easily in his arms. Laughing, they crossed the threshold, ready to begin their new lives.

**WATCH FOR
6 NEW TITLES EVERY MONTH!**

## Second Chance at Love

## WATCH FOR
## 6 NEW TITLES EVERY MONTH!

# Second Chance at Love

All of the above titles are $1.75 per copy

# WATCH FOR
# 6 NEW TITLES EVERY MONTH!

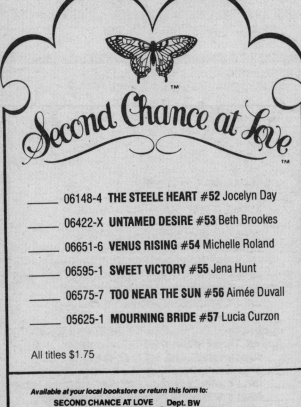

## Second Chance at Love

_____ 06148-4 **THE STEELE HEART #52** Jocelyn Day

_____ 06422-X **UNTAMED DESIRE #53** Beth Brookes

_____ 06651-6 **VENUS RISING #54** Michelle Roland

_____ 06595-1 **SWEET VICTORY #55** Jena Hunt

_____ 06575-7 **TOO NEAR THE SUN #56** Aimée Duvall

_____ 05625-1 **MOURNING BRIDE #57** Lucia Curzon

All titles $1.75